## Praise for *Ahalya*

'Ahalya, Draupadi, Kunti, Tara, Mandodari – each of the Pancha Kanyas is fascinating. Ahalya's story has been told and retold several times, sometimes with varying accounts across texts. What was her relationship with Gautam and Indra? What was her crime? How was she redeemed? Why is she among the Pancha Kanyas? There have been modern retellings and interpretations too. Koral Dasgupta's wonderful retelling adds to this corpus, with a lyrical and poetic quality. The image that will remain with you is of the Mist ... Enthralling'

**Bibek Debroy**

'"Go, woman, find your world yourself. The joy you seek deserves to be discovered." Armed with this advice, Ahalya sets off on her life's journey. The magical and thought-provoking adventure that follows will intrigue and mesmerize readers'

**Chitra Banerjee Divakaruni**

'Koral Dasgupta's evocation of Ahalya, the first of the Pancha Kanyas, the five virtuous women from Indian myth, is an enigmatic tale about purity, chastity, seduction and redemption, told from the perspective of the eternal feminine'

**Namita Gokhale**

'Amazing premise and approach. This is one unique take on an age-old tale. Brilliant and intriguing'

**Anand Neelakantan**

'Impressed. I literally never imagined the interior world of a character from mythology in this way, let alone contemplating this way of reflecting on the soul, embodiment, desire and a woman's experience of the Brahma- and Indra-dominated worlds! Really powerful'

**Prof Brian A. Hatcher**

'In this original and spirited interpretation of the tale of Ahalya, Koral Dasgupta gives voice, character and agency to an enigmatic and fascinating female figure from ancient Hindu lore, while exploring and seeking to resolve the proverbial and vexing tension between asceticism and sensuality'

**Prof Philip Lutgendorf**

'Engaging and cinematic narrative'

**Srijit Mukherjee**

'A stream of consciousness; a spiritual telling. It rescued and redeemed the purity ruse. Koral is a visual writer'

**Nabila Jamshed**

'A stunning read. Fluent and engaging. What a fine writer!'

**Fiona Sampson**

'Panchakanya and other women, reinterpreted, is a most pertinent call. *Ahalya* is beautifully written and the little details and imagined conversations bring the character alive. I also enjoyed the almost surrealistic movement between mythical time and ours. It's a reminder that we in India live by a philosophy of transitions, an in-between-ness. Ahalya is amongst us'

**Prof Malashri Lal**

'Powerful ... The novelty of the novel lies in the fact that no other writer has talked about Ahalya vis-à-vis her womanhood'

***Outlook***

'In a most intriguing retelling, Dasgupta's narrative turns the seduction story on its head, making Ahalya the seducer instead of the seduced'

***Scroll.in***

'An ecocritical reading of *Ahalya* reveals the exploration of an ancient connection with nature that's sacred, intimate, and as we are in the midst of an environmental emergency, vital to reconcile with today'

***Firstpost***

'[T]he brilliance of Dasgupta's retelling is not just within the confines of that transformation itself, but rather, the importance of being seen, validated and loved as you are'

***Southern Humanities Review***

'Koral Dasgupta creates true wonder with her new book *Ahalya*'

***Tempest***

'A stunning piece of literature'

**Dipannita Sharma**

## Praise for *Kunti*

'Koral Dasgupta writes about Kunti, one of the Pancha Kanyas, with verve, emotion and passion. Her highly readable account of this fascinating character, who played a key role in the Mahabharata, is a must for those wishing to know about our past and the dialectics of gender within it'

**Pavan K. Varma**

'Koral Dasgupta makes the ancient myths speak in new and unexpected voices; voices that have been lost and sunken in the dominant narrative consciousness, and yet, the voices of characters who made the flesh, blood and the values of the epics possible'

**Saikat Majumdar**

'Bringing heroines of yore, like Ahalya and Kunti, to contemporary times, Koral Dasgupta writes with a rare verve and energy. Never dull or pedantic, she makes the woman within the legend come alive. A rare talent'

**Makarand R. Paranjape**

## Praise for *Draupadi*

'*Draupadi* lives up to the expectations set by *Ahalya* and *Kunti* ... Koral [Dasgupta] dares to boldly push the narrative in ways you cannot imagine. A must-read'

**Kiran Manral**

'This is a striking rewriting of Draupadi's story. Koral Dasgupta has given us a Draupadi who is fearless, politically astute and unwilling to be anyone's victim. This Draupadi leans into her power and changes the course of history in Dasgupta's beautifully crafted world'

**Prof Tracy Pintchman**

'In poetic prose Koral Dasgupta weaves surprising threads into the ever-evolving tapestry of the Mahabharata, enriching it with this empowering, lyrical telling of Draupadi's life'

**Prof Hillary P. Rodrigues**

'Koral Dasgupta has given us a unique take on a well-known story from the Mahabharata. It is fascinating to hear this tale from a female perspective, to hear [Draupadi's] thoughts and struggles about being offered in marriage to all five brothers, as well as her eventual realization of the purpose behind the marriage. This work clearly shows Draupadi to be an intelligent and rational player in the divine plan. In our attempts to make the academic world more diverse and accessible to all, a reading of Draupadi alongside the Mahabharata would be an excellent way to open new dialogues in the classroom and beyond'

**Prof Arnold Smit**

'This lyrical and insightful reimagining of Draupadī's narrative is a worthy entry in the long tradition of telling the tales of India's (and the world's) great epics'

**Prof Brian Collins**

'A lively series of beloved stories from ancient India that speak to modern readers'

**Prof Paul B. Courtright**

## Praise for *Mandodari*

'Imaginative, intense and insightful ... Narrated in Koral's signature style, the exchanges of Mandodari and Sita (and their implications for Ravan and Ram) are absolutely fascinating'

**Ashwin Sanghi**

'[*Mandodari*] has several strengths, including, but not limited to, Dasgupta's envisioning of the inner world of the women of Lanka, the differences, sympathies and alliances within, as well as the titular character's moral turbulence'

***Telegraph***

'*Mandodari* with its lyrical prose and philosophical moorings ... conjures up visions of a mesmerizing world. The book shows how so much is made possible by a lone woman's resilience and unswerving commitment to do the right thing'

***New Indian Express***

## Praise for *Tara*

'Embedded within the epic saga of the Ramayan, *Tara*'s nuanced narrative is bathed in grace and empathy. We enter the non-textual world of the vanaras to discover a deep worldview through the voice of an extraordinary protagonist'

**Namita Gokhale**

'A powerful depiction of Tara's world, encompassing Bali and Sugreev, with distinct ideologies influencing the rules of the Kishkindha kingdom'

**Amish**

'Exuberant and imaginative, this narrative about kinship, friendship and love explores questions about borders: between the animal and the human, the wild and the tame, the living and the dead, the revelatory and the remembered, heaven and earth, language and silence. With a cast of vividly etched characters and a feel for the mysteries that lie at the heart of intimacy, here is a fascinating tale by an inventive and thoughtful storyteller'

**Arundhathi Subramaniam**

# MANDODARI

KORAL DASGUPTA has published an eclectic range of books, from academic non-fiction to relationship dramas. Her books are discussed in the context of gender studies, art, myth and ecocritical literature. Other than India, Koral's books can be found in the libraries of Harvard University, Columbia University, the University of Pennsylvania, University of Chicago, University of Wales, Duke University, University of North Carolina, Texas A&M University, among others. The books in the Sati series have been nominated for various prestigious awards, with *Ahalya* most recently being recommended for the 2023 Sahitya Akademi Prize Honour List.

Koral is the founder of www.tellmeyourstory.biz and conducts writing programmes and critical thinking workshops for educational and corporate floors. She has been recognized on the Innovator25 Asia Pacific 2019 list prepared by the Holmes Report and featured in the Women of Wonder (WOW) series in *Outlook Business* magazine.

Her website is www.koraldasgupta.com.

**Also in the Sati series**

*Ahalya*

*Kunti*

*Draupadi*

*Tara*

# MANDODARI

KORAL DASGUPTA

THE SATI SERIES IV

PAN

First published 2023 by Pan
An imprint of Pan Macmillan Publishing India Private Limited
707 Kailash Building
26 K. G. Marg, New Delhi 110001
www.panmacmillan.co.in

Pan Macmillan, The Smithson, 6 Briset Street Farringdon, London EC1M 5NR
Associated companies throughout the world
www.panmacmillan.com

ISBN 978-93-95624-70-1



9 8



Typeset in Guardi LT Std by R. Ajith Kumar, New Delhi
Printed and bound at Repro India Limited

FSC www.fsc.org
MIX
Paper | Supporting responsible forestry
FSC® C047271

*For my son, Neev Tanish*

# CONTENTS

## SERIES INTRODUCTION

The Pancha Kanyas of Hindu mythology are Ahalya, Kunti, Draupadi, Mandodari and Tara, while the five Satis include Sita, Sati, Savitri, Damayanti and Arundhati. The distinction between these two different titles arose primarily because certain versions of the epics have taken the liberty to celebrate women as per the popular beliefs of their era and, of course, those of the translators. One school of thought defines 'Sati' as symbolizing the women's unconditional devotion to and dependence on their men. It casts the women as loyal followers, strongly supporting the vision of the men around them or helping them overcome social and emotional challenges. These women are depicted as self-sacrificing and selfless, yet invincible when drafting their own position of strength and authority.

Various senior scholars translate the Pancha Kanyas as 'five virgins'. Thus, based on textual evidence, the Kanyas and Satis are different women. However, in the earliest texts, there is no mention of the Pancha Satis; they only talk about the Pancha Kanyas who are deemed as the Maha Satis. Even in regional interpretations, especially in some eastern and southern states of the country, this division is blurred. This could be due to the difference in the spread of the Mahabharat of Vedavyasa versus the dissemination of Valmiki Ramayan. The former specifically mentions the Pancha Kanyas.

Many versions of the Ramayan discuss the Satis in terms of loyalty and physical chastity. Such women, including Sita, aren't restricted to only five. But they don't club them under the umbrella term, Pancha Sati. In my own studies, I came across some scholarly assumptions that the Satis were reborn as Kanyas, with research trying to draw parallels!

An ancient *shloka* establishes that reciting the names of the Pancha Kanya can dispel sins, which again confirms the 'Sati' status of these women. Sati, meaning pure, devoted and fair. Purity that cannot be destroyed by external influence, because criticism or judgment cannot deflect one from her chosen path of righteousness.

In the Sati series, I follow this conception of 'purity' while retelling the stories of the five illustrious women: Ahalya, Kunti, Draupadi, Mandodari and Tara. The purity that is brave enough to present itself the way it is – sans any cosmetic cover – and mirrors the mind unpretentiously as much as it exposes the politics of a society.

However, the Sati series is not meant to be biographical. The purpose of the series is to draw attention to a part of the journeys of these legendary women that have been grossly overlooked. Identities have been imposed based on incidents that the patriarchy considered criminal, shameful or irresponsible. When these known events adopt the narrative voice of a feminine titular character, the stories change. The world expands. The Sati series not only presents an inclusive overview of the protagonist's own life but also dives deep into the suppressed pain of those around them – be it a man or a woman.

In the first, fourth and fifth book of the series, *Ahalya, Mandodari* and *Tara,* the entire narrative had to be recreated. About Kunti and Draupadi, a lot is known already. My retellings spotlight the making of these characters, albeit from a non-traditional perspective, which ushers the readers into a new era of thinking and reimagining.

*Ahalya* introduced the woman as a lover. Ambitious, futuristic, royal and calculative; not afraid to express, nor hesitant to ignore the binding rules of the world. *Kunti* called for a relook at the patriarchal origins of 'Mata' and, in relation, the pervasive sociopolitical image of the sacrificing Indian mother. *Draupadi* was even more complicated than the previous books because it shed light on the societal reactions across generations towards crimes against women, particularly those who are successful. *Mandodari* sparked yet another powerful discourse on the critical choices faced by an accomplished woman between the calls of of her mind and heart, in light of a terrible sin committed by her extremely talented husband. *Tara,* the last book of the series, brings up the discourse of human–animal politics, highlighting the grandeur of certain traditions of the forest and the wisdom of animals that transcends boundaries. It also explores the sensitivity that prompts a woman to forgo the blinds borne by the diplomatic crown of a queen.

Ram's killing of Bali while hiding behind a bush is a disturbing episode from the Ramayan that I personally could never digest. Tara's narrative opens with an acknowledgement of Bali's death and then travels through the sequence of events – securing some emotional and logical derivatives.

# PROLOGUE

On the darkest of nights, when everyone was asleep, the sea was awake. The jingle of multi-layered anklets resounded through the black sandstone stairs of the commanding edifice, in absolute disharmony with the echo of turbulent waves. The creatures of the sea looked up. Into the playful water where my feet were immersed, I dropped a few grains. The greedy red fish lapped them up. Before moving away, they deftly cleaned with their tail the slippery algae coating the lower steps. A blue mountain of granite, cobalt spinel and silica rooted deep within the sea spread its generous hue, cradling a mystical prison in its womb.

I couldn't see well in the darkness. Only a vague masculine frame was visible, his neck and body confined with thick iron chains against the wall. A part of the torso was above water. Beneath, slimy creatures wrapped around his waist and legs. The raging waves churned fog and foam. A wispy curtain of smoke denied the pleasure of determining how intimidated he was by my ghastly prison.

Many flights of steps had brought me to this vestibule. Each layer I left behind returned my excitement with congratulatory applause. Fire danced on the walls from earthen holders. The path gleamed with distorted seashells inscribed graphically, petrifying the ripples with their reflections. Every corner of Lanka rejoiced at the incarceration of the chronic menace abhorred by their glorious monarch, finally handcuffed after many failed wars.

I had specially prepared for this meeting. The finest gold adorned my hands and waist. My drape was woven with rare threads sourced from ace artisans across the country. I was the queen of the land. And he, no more than a lowly prisoner. Indra was the captive of my son Meghnad, now known as Indrajit!

'Welcome to Lanka,' I said with a smirk, standing on the stairs. 'This humble earthly prison is honoured to host the Devraj.'

The metallic chain clanged against the wall as Indra made an effort to look up. After a pregnant pause, his voice lashed like the baffled waves. 'In the mortal and immortal worlds, nothing is permanent.'

Ah! Indra was trying to pull me into his illusion. What else could he do? I was not falling into that maze. Neither would I allow him to dismiss his defeat.

'Mortal and immortal worlds! Well said, Devraj.' It was fun to call him 'Devraj' again and again. Why should I not? Hadn't Indra and his privileged clan always been dismissive and sarcastic towards a large section of us Mortals? I wanted to insult our prisoner. His snobbery, born out of the celestial throne, was known to prick the pride of many young talents attempting to uncover their brilliance. 'Everything on earth is black or white, good or bad, sinful or virtuous, *dharma* or *adharma*. In the immortal world, however, the rules are reversed. Everything unfair is a philosophical metaphor – glorified as the magnificence of the Divine. A toxic discrimination distances the essence of existence. Yet, fools continue to pray.'

The iron chains must be hurting. Indra craned his neck to take a proper look at me. I could feel his eyes traversing my body. Expecting a lewd remark, my right toe was ready for action. One signal to the automated system would compress the place, bringing the thick walls closer to Indra, shrinking further his already compromised comfort. But the prisoner restrained, unlike the lech I had expected him to be.

'Is this you or Ravan speaking?' he asked, astonished. 'Queen Mandodari, I respect your love for Dashanan. But I don't understand your blind support for his stubborn irrationality!'

'Do yourself a favour and don't ever try to understand,' I blurted out. Was this

Immortal remotely qualified to comprehend the unfathomable? These silly beings didn't know the language of splurging or preserving. They couldn't love completely; they didn't know hatred either. The Immortals evaluated actions on the scale of rewards and punishments. Punishments that often targeted not only the offender but also the fraternity, whether or not they were at fault.

'Explain, Queen Mandodari,' Indra pressed on. 'I want to understand this love. Why do you partner with an abusive king? How did you lose your logic to the Lankan coasts? Is Ravan that wonderful a husband?'

I looked down at the sea where a swarm of creatures had flocked, splashing water with their tails and releasing bubbles through their gills. I threw the grains in my palms at them. They dispersed. Where was the haughty Indra, for whom I had come to the sea all the way from my palace? Was this even Indra? I had come to further destroy the one whom my son, Meghnad, had conquered. He was guilty of being Ravan's biggest enemy.

'Who are you? You don't seem like Indra,' I uttered, wondering if Meghnad had been tricked.

'Who do you think is Indra?'

Here, this was the playful tenor typical of the Devraj. Before I could thwart his ramblings, the music in his voice whipped across the water. 'Indra is an illusion, queen. Indra is your impulse. Nebulous, undefined. How you perceive him is reflective of your character, not Indra's. It will take a lot from you to analyse the other world with mortal consciousness.'

I frowned. Through the clear ocean water of the night, lit up only by the flickering torch hanging from the high roof, I could see large fish gobbling up smaller ones. The huge universe was ridiculously enclosed within this tiny truth. The smaller fish would be swallowed by the larger ones, leaving behind bubbles in the memory of the deceased, which would eventually burst. The ultimate battle is to ascertain who is the smaller fish, what bubble it can create and how long will the bubble sustain! The mortal world is that simple. In my heart, I agreed that Indra's immortal world, where no one dies, would be far too complicated.

Should this imply that Mortals cannot attempt to untangle the complications? Why was access restricted? The agitation had disappeared for a while, it was coming back again. Ravan's battle, and mine with him, was against the entitlements of the immortal world, which deprived the talents everywhere else.

'I am a master illusionist too, in case you have forgotten. From me has Indrajit,' I relished calling Meghnad by the new name, 'inherited his power of illusion that could defeat Indra's.'

Startled by so many simultaneous attacks, Indra kept quiet before laughing his heart out, irritating me further and sending the marine creatures to clash against each other in their hurry to rush out. 'Queen, you have only imprisoned Devraj, the keeper of Indralok. Indra still resides in your senses, in your love for Ravan, in his arrogance and in the way you both view the world – aligned yet distinct. That Indra will always be free.'

I clenched my teeth. He was right. Why else would I feel this intense frustration brewing inside? Even if I killed Indra right now, he'd still be alive. Such were the perks of the Immortals. Mortals could object, but the objection would be overruled. Challenging the order was supposedly self-destructive.

Intimidations motivated Ravan. He refused to give in; I refused to leave him alone. We had vowed to walk through this fire together, whatever it took.

This anger could be a trap!

I rubbed my hands against my arms to calm myself. Indra shouldn't overpower me. After a few moments, I smiled.

'The earth has a paradise of its own, Devraj. I have created it. It is called Lanka. The country exemplifies a fantastic fusion of the Asur excellence in making profitable use of nature. Here the residents are not reminded every day that nature is more powerful. Hierarchy prevails based on aptitude. A labourer is distanced from the king, but we are united as a clan.'

'What is your friction with nature, Queen Mandodari?' Indra sounded frustrated.

'We have nothing against nature, Devraj. Our friction is with the Immortals who have acquired complete possession of nature and inflicted the earth with consequences every time there is disobedience,' I slashed his superiority.

'Agreed that the Immortals control nature. But who bears the fruits?' He tried to sound generous.

I laughed at his political chicanery. 'Nature should report to both the mortal and immortal worlds. Come share the responsibility. We are happy to share the fruits.'

'Immortals are not unfair, queen,' Indra said grimly. 'We retaliate only when the Mortals fiddle with nature to an extent that it merits punishment.'

'Who are you to punish?' I thrust upon him. 'Brahma created both Mortals and Immortals. If the design merits unequal privileges for either, then that design is flawed and the designer partial.'

'You believe Brahma is biased?' Indra fired back. 'Is that why you decided to penalize nature?'

'Penalize? No, we don't intend to penalize. We are on our onward journey. We created our industries, developed our centres of science and innovation. We expect the nature to cooperate, instead of feeling insecure,' I snapped at him again.

This time, Indra remained silent, perhaps lining up the next round of negotiations. There were none left.

'Why do you question the established rituals of the *Brahmand*? What will you get out of this?' he asked finally.

How long I had waited for this question. I had even rehearsed my response, expecting this opportunity. 'We believe Ravan is far more deserving of reigning over the cosmic systems than Indra,' I said slowly. 'If Ravan rules, destiny will be well-governed, and more people will be happy. Step down, Devraj, for fresh lessons in administration, to bind the cosmos into a preferred discipline. Will you?'

My proposal amused him. 'How, Queen Mandodari?' Indra's voice mixed with the battering of the waves. 'Ravan Raj prioritizes Ravan above all else. Is self-obsession a trait of good leadership?'

'Impulse. Isn't that what you claimed to be?' I countered. 'The impulse resulting from the five senses has landed you in trouble so many times. The sixth sense, Vishnu, steps in each time to clear the mess.' I pointed a finger at him. 'You need to include others because of your own shortcomings. Ravan does not. He is capable of defending all on his own.'

'Defend! You must be joking.' Indra breathed heavily. An eerie gust of moist air coiled between us. 'In the mortal world, everything is perishable, Queen Mandodari. Lanka, your creative haven, will also perish. Time is ruthless. But Ravan's blunders will demolish your fond artistry well in advance.'

'Time is kind,' I argued. 'Time doesn't discriminate. Whether it is you or me, Ravan or Meghnad – time will turn for all.'

Indra's shackles clanged again with impatience. 'Time affects the terrestrial in one way and the celestial in another. Mahadev is the universal source of strength for both Mortals and Immortals. The beings of both worlds circumambulate his orbit. The Immortals are capable of sucking more energy at a time. Fighting this is futile. You gain nothing, spend everything and are not even left with yourself for company.'

Devraj never stopped discouraging. I never stopped refuting.

'We will continue our fight against your prejudice,' I announced brazenly. 'We are ready for the ugliest form of sacrifice. History will be compelled to document that one mortal did not bow before the supremacy of the Immortals. We may not win. What will sting the world forever is that we refused to accept defeat.'

# 1

'Ram Rajya!' I heard her saying with great conviction. 'Someday, Trijata, you will be sitting in Lanka, listening to the people of Ayodhya cheering for Ram Rajya.' It sounded like a chant in a small temple where the deity was missing, but the priest kept serving.

'Ram Rajya?' Trijata repeated. 'I don't hear any mention of Sita in that one-track title.'

She didn't fall for the provocation.

'Ram Rajya is not an ideology to please its founder, rather a proposed path for people to willingly walk through and attain bliss.' The petite face of the slender captive in Lanka was shining like an opulent queen's. 'It is exactly as it sounds. A brief poetry. Not an equity for the entitled. Ram Rajya will spread its splendour, whether or not I am in this world to witness it.'

Trijata scolded her for her choice of words. 'What kind of woman dreams of something she won't live to see? Plans may fail, fair woman; thoughts seldom do.'

There was a strange bond between these two souls from two different parts of the earth. I had seldom seen their thoughts match. Nonetheless, the warmth was evident. When others weren't watching, Trijata looked northwards and nodded. Once again, I walked away from Ashok Vatika, without meeting Sita.

I don't know why I went there. There was always an unexplainable urge to see her from a distance. I went at a time when the gatekeepers would relax, leaving everything to Trijata. With her around, no one had any concern. She wasn't Ravan's favourite for nothing. Oddly, though, she was Sita's favourite too.

It was a morning of high tide when Sita entered Ashok Vatika. Waves peaked and fell inauspiciously, as if a storm was looming. Little sea animals were thrown ashore and not pulled back into the water. Their shells scattered around, still protecting the dead bodies. The sun had set, the water was raging. Two of our scheduled trade ships postponed their departure. The sparrow's nest fell from the vestibule, breaking the eggs. A nauseating fetor pervaded in from the rear window, under which the Rakshasis had gathered to taunt the captive. One of them touched Sita's hand with the tip of her finger. 'She seems like a ball of sugar. Don't let her in the pool, she will melt.' The Rakshasi burst into laughter. Sita was not amused by the touch, which inspired them to instigate her more.

'Look at her hair. So soft and straight!' another commented. 'Where are the curls? Did the elephants walk on your mane while you were sleeping?' She was not done yet; her companion pushed her. 'Only the hair? Look at her nails. So small, it's almost as though she has none. Rats must have feasted on them at night.'

They both fell upon each other, laughing. If words weren't enough, Sita was being pushed and pulled in all directions. Unsolicited observations and unwelcome gestures pricked her. Another lady erupted, 'How could you miss her complexion? The naughty forest-god has licked the woman's body off its colour while her husband was away.'

'She has had a lot of fun with the forest being uninhabited and a too-trusting husband.' They chuckled. Sita cringed at the scandalous gossip. Her frail body dropped to the ground unconscious, tired of resisting.

This was when a curt voice tore apart the jeers of the bullies. 'Should I tell Queen Mandodari what the women in her backyard think about straight hair and fair skin?'

The critics in Ashok Vatika fled upon spotting Trijata. The young woman lifted Sita by her hands and sprinkled water on her face, nurturing her back to strength.

*

This part of the world was populated by large-bodied inhabitants with broad features. They looked different from the land where I lived with my father, Mayasur. The skin was dark here, and rough like sand. Elongated eyes stretched till the ears, eyelashes were longer and ears hung down to the shoulders. Oily scalps cultivated thick hair – curly and entangled. Voices were loud and shrill, like the sound of brass utensils falling to the floor. The average height was higher than what I was accustomed to before I married Ravan. Other than gold, the royals adorned their necks and hair with seashells and pearls. The ideals of beauty were conflicting.

Men wore precious stones around their necks and embraced rugged body odours. The stronger the odour, the more masculine they were considered, their appeal putting to shame all who were comparatively deodorized!

Ravan's sister, Meenakshi, a prolific diva of the land, was arrogant and condescending, like the glamorous usually are. Every morning, the bathing pool was readied with petals and pollens of wild flowers floating in coconut water. No one was permitted to step inside till Meenakshi had finished her elaborate regimen for the day. Before diving into the pool, she would sit in the tree shade, grooming her long, pointed nails. She massaged them regularly with potions prepared in her kitchen using ingredients best known to herself. Her fascination with the dagger-like nails had earned her a nickname, 'Surpnakha'. It was an unspoken rule to not disturb Meenakshi during her morning routine. Her arms, back and shoulders flaunted cryptic symbols of the Asurs. The gold paint bordering white shone against her dark skin. I had touched them once out of curiosity when she had just stepped out of the bath and the pool was being prepared for me. She swivelled in shock and jumped back into the pool, rubbing her fingers over the spot as if I had smeared muck on it.

I thought the Rakshasis were ugly; they thought I was.

When the girls made fun of Sita at Ashok Vatika, I heard everything they wanted to say to their queen but couldn't!

*

On the pedestal below Sita's sat Trijata, their fingers entwined. Sita spoke about the Ram Rajya that she and her husband were to build together. It was their labour of love. This aspirational castle had laid its foundation over the last thirteen years of their exile.

'What is this Ram Rajya you are so fascinated by?' Trijata crushed pomegranates between her palms and ran them through her open hair before tucking it into a bun. Thin red streaks peeked between the strands.

'It is a unique statesmanship to empower and unite the people of Ayodhya,' Sita's voice was feeble but firm. 'The subjects here would live without fear or hesitation, with dignity and education ...'

Trijata was bewildered. 'What are you saying, woman! You want your subjects to live without fear of their king? They will do anything they want and you wouldn't know how to cast them off.'

Trijata's concern was justified. Even my brows had furrowed. A mynah sang from above, hiding behind one of the branches.

'I said without fear. Not without love,' Sita explained warmly. 'If they love, they will respect.'

My gaze lifted above into the leaves, trying to locate the mynah. Everyone who heard the mynah could assume that the bird was eager to entertain its audience. But the mynah sings because singing is its character. Can anyone motivate the bird for a repeat performance? Impractical expectations lead to disappointments. However, Sita was willing to die protecting this illusive metaphor called Ram Rajya.

'You really believe in this word, *love,* no? Ram's love for you. People's love for Ram–Sita. The love and harmony among the people of Ram Rajya.' Trijata smiled.

'You don't?' Sita's question was simple, but Trijata was stumped.

'No, we don't. We understand affection. The rest are principles and duties that no one is allowed to override. When discipline fails, there is a penalty. We believe that mutual affection lasts till neither the receiver nor the giver is threatened. Love is overrated.'

Trijata's explanation silenced Sita. It got me thinking too. Everyone in this country was taught the laws from a very young age. Even casual conversations were laced with words lifted straight from the constitution. No one could violate it. The king amended the rulebook as per evolving preferences and morals. The subjects went back to memorize the amended rules.

I would often watch her from my bedside window. Sita sat with her back against the base of the shimshapa tree. I seldom saw her resting. All day long she remained preoccupied, obsessing over her ideology. Passion crumbles into shards of broken glass if one is not empirical enough to identify and revise the follies. Follies are many, in everything. Who would explain this to Sita? Her faith had been her only solace since Ravan had separated her from Ram.

She was looking skywards, singing her poetry. Sita's voice was not that of a trained vocalist. The rugged, oral composition burned and broke the surface of the earth. It quaked with her truth, shaking the foundations of the lavish palace that sprawled many floors below the ground, while majestic staircases spiralled towards the sky. Ravan wanted his palace in Lanka to be as enormous as Mount Kailash, and his woman in its chambers to resemble a thousand goddesses.

There was a vast difference between my worship and Ravan's. I followed Shankar; Ravan was a devotee of Maheshwar. I submitted to the power, he competed with it.

Did Sita expect the winds of Lanka to carry her poetry to Ram? Unlikely. The rowdy winds had a roar of their own. They would drown her voice in the ocean rather than acting as her messenger. Everyone in Lanka reported to Ravan, even the winds. This captive woman was the only contradiction.

Why did she sing? To irk Ravan? Again, unlikely. She didn't do anything for Ravan. It was another matter altogether that the king couldn't stand her music. Fearlessness can unnerve the sharpest swords.

The lyrics painted a portrait of the forthcoming Ram Rajya. A delightful country with bounteous rivers, broad paddy fields beside them, well-grown husks waiting to be milled, cheerful people and healthy cattle. Abundance in thoughts and deeds. Where the king of Ayodhya would sit with the peasants on a level ground. Her eyes were filled with an unrealistic fantasy that didn't consider the strategic estimation underlying enterprising programmes. Adversities must be predicted in advance. Else, innocence gets trapped within undue controversies.

Sita's tune was replete with the joys of motherhood. In her mind, she had adopted Ayodhya as her child. The songs promised protection and sustenance to her subjects, envisioning alliances leading to employment and expansion. She included her brothers-in-law – Lakshman, Bharat and Shatrughan – in her resource allocations. Wasn't it Bharat's mother who conspired their banishment so that her son could become king? Sita was quite oblivious to political choreographies. Poor woman! She was too forgiving, nice and naïve.

With a thud, I shut the huge window that opened to Ashok Vatika. Watching Sita was inspiring at times, depressing otherwise. I stepped backwards only to bump against a cold chest. Huge ruby and emeralds held together by gigantic gold threads needled my spine. Though turned away, I could feel Ravan's agitation.

'What attracts you to Sita?' He made no attempts to conceal his displeasure.

'Me!' I exclaimed.

'Don't hide it, queen. You keep a watch on her all the time. When you miss an hour of her day, Trijata fills you in. Why?'

It was impossible to keep anything from Ravan as long as I stood on the soil of Lanka. I tried to walk past him. He grabbed my arm and pulled me towards himself. Raising my head with his finger on my chin, he looked into my eyes to read something unspoken.

'Why do you bother, Mandodari? This woman is nobody in our world. I am speaking the truth,' he whispered in angst. 'Listen to me, queen. She is only a passing desire, no different from many others, born to serve the masters and die thereafter. No one will ever take your place.'

Ravan could be this direct. My smile invited a tense frown.

'Who said I am possessive of my treasure?'

Ravan's tight grip loosened, leaving a blue mark on my arm. I turned to leave, gently nursing the affected spot with my finger. Before I could move, his hand fell around my neck like iron shackles.

'What did you just say? Repeat.' His voice was shaking with anger. I could also sense pain. Ravan drew me to himself, his cheeks brushing up against my hair. This used to feel romantic till a few days ago, when I would run my fingers tenderly over his hands, one girdling my neck and the other around my waist. I would take off his large wrist bands and untie his armlets. He would drop the enormous ornament hanging down his neck. On his return from his expeditions, Ravan would bring samples of tree barks and beautiful stones for my collection. It was my childhood hobby to store architectural elements of the earth in jars and bowls for my personal study. Those were different days from another time.

'Set her free. Return her to Ram.' My voice choked. 'She is bad company for Lanka.'

I could feel Ravan's jaws tightening. 'Even Ram may not want her back as badly as you seek their reunion,' he dismissed. 'Stop thinking about Sita. She and her people are no more than tough mud waiting to be crushed beneath my heels. I will do that in style so they remember their boundaries.'

A crash from behind startled us. Cold water touched my ankle and wriggled forward. Something slimy and soft was kicked aside. Ah, the lotus pot must have been in his way.

'A cyclone builds in her breath,' I continued to warn. 'It will shatter the tallest and strongest pillars of Lanka. The pillars that were your vision and my art.'

Lately, I've had too many nightmares about a dilapidated Lanka, the golden country destroyed by the advent of invaders. Ravan had always valued my intuitions. This time, he was strangely distanced and unbending. I didn't know how to bring him back. The presence of Sita had affected our relationship. 'As long as she is here, I feel like a hostage too.' I shuddered, looking at the closed window through which Sita's songs permeated into my chamber.

'Shift yourself elsewhere in the palace. Choose the quarters that are farthest from Ashok Vatika.' Ravan wanted me to stop. I wish I could.

'Not looking at the problem is hardly a solution,' I retorted.

Finally, he pushed me away with great force and stormed out. I fell to the ground. Sarama walked in after a while to light the evening lamp and put back in order whatever Ravan had scattered. The younger sister-in-law, she wiped the floor and picked up the broken pieces of the pot, along with trampled remains of the soft lotus petals. By my bedside, she set a silver bowl and left a water lily afloat on its surface. Gently, she touched my head and motioned for me to rise. A warm blend of sunflower and coconut oils were applied over my neck and arms with the tip of her fingers. In the mirror in front of us, she caught me staring at the majestic lily.

'Isn't it beautiful?' she gushed, her palm running all over my hand. The bluish bruise had subsided considerably.

'A few mornings ago, I went for a bath in the pool beside the temple,' I recollected. 'It was quieter there. Ravan's melodic morning chants resounded all over the place. One lotus swayed to his verses. Mesmerized by his voice and rhythm, it danced forward – as if possessed, to reach the end of the pond. It bent its stem to listen to his hymns as intently as it could.' Sarama's hands stilled on my elbow. 'Charmed by this generous admirer, I picked it up and brought it here. Ravan destroyed that lotus this evening. Please inform him.'

Sarama got up quickly to complete the chores she had left unattended. She wouldn't say a word to Ravan. She wouldn't have to. Ravan was around somewhere, listening to our conversation. A response would come to us in some way or another, either to please us or to shock, at a time suitable to him.

## 2

Those were the days when I was new to Lanka. During one of my trips to the western part of the country, I asked for the palanquin to be lowered.

'Push aside, silly shadows should not dare to cloud the king's way!' The little ones clapped. They had hung colourful clothes in shades of red, green and violet from the branches of the trees. The ends of the clothes brushed the ground like props in the royal court. I smiled, watching from behind a small Shiva temple.

'No mercy for Kuber!' screamed one, raising a wooden plank shaped like a sword. The others repeated after him. 'Until the end and forever with Ravan.' Another one, smaller and weaker than the others, jumped down from a branch, bringing down an orange drape with him.

'Catch the enemy! Swords out, everyone.' The others charged at him. The poor child was not convinced in his role as Kuber; he must have been bullied to play the villain. Very quickly, he allowed himself to be defeated by the king's men and ran away.

'Long live Ravan, the king of kings! No world beyond Lankesh.'

I burst into silent laughter, wondering if they knew anything about Kuber at all. Or were they conveniently calling him an enemy because he had been defeated by Ravan? The child Ravan, who owned the wooden sword, swirled his toy above his head. Those he favoured were the generals in Ravan's army. The unpopular one had to settle as Kuber. The power plays begin quite early in life.

Kuber, Ravan's half-brother, was also the keeper of wealth. The assets accumulated during his reign graced the land of Lanka with opulence.

I had never met him. No one spoke about Kuber. During one of my northward travels, I was warned about the forbidden grounds. I descended from the palanquin and walked briefly while the bearers rested. Old Tillana, my personal attendant and chief palanquin-runner, followed from a distance. It was a large, open area with lots of trees and pools. The trees had parts of their bark peeled off. Large tortoises with Yantra symbols on their backs were lazing on the soil. They jumped into the water and disappeared when they spotted me.

I would have crossed the rocky fences bordering the expanse if Tillana had not stopped me. 'Why?' I asked. The desolate grassland was enticing. A sultry breeze flirted with the tourists. All I could make from Tillana's mumble was 'curses of the Yaksha'! He would not say more. Fascinating was the humour of life. Between adventure and the lack of it, the choice was obvious. Tillana scratched his head, screening the surroundings fearfully. The queen was adamant about her recce. If she did not quit her mission, the king would greet him at swordpoint. After much deliberation, Tillana secured a promise of confidentiality from me.

'Those are the symbols of Kuber on the tortoise shells. Once upon a time, they moved around with pride, like the brahmins among animals. The Yaksha's emblem bejewelled their backs. Kuber treated them like his children while the others stared in awe. Many of the trees carried his Yantra too. His shrines were scattered here and there. Ravan's rule has demolished all and reconstructed a lot. The cruel Kuber's hidden treasure has been unearthed. The kingdom has been cleansed of all remnants of the erstwhile monarch. We uprooted and replanted the forest. Yet, the fresh undergrowth on these terrains carries his unlucky signature.' Frustration gathered in droplets on Tillana's neck and forehead.

The soil will need some investigation – I made a mental note. Researchers should be able to deduce the composition of the fertilizers Kuber applied to this land. I bent down to scoop a little in my hand. Tillana was almost on the verge of crying. He pleaded that I refrain from touching the doomed grounds. I rolled my eyes and withdrew.

'The king sends woodcutters to peel off the barks from time to time,' I was told. 'It is believed that this part of the land is jinxed. No one comes here. We must leave, queen.'

'Was Kuber cruel?' I wanted to extract more information.

'He must be. How can the enemy be a good person?' Tillana pronounced nervously, eager to pick up the palanquin on his shoulder.

'And the tortoises?' I probed, disregarding his worries.

'Those are ghosts of the past, queen. Many tortoises have been killed. Ravan's land does not appreciate the presence of Kuber's pets. But some still escape and breed to come back and flaunt their shells. Obnoxious creatures!' he blasted at them.

Ghosts of the past, indeed. If one remained quiet, the murmur of the leaves here tried to tell a story in a language that no one understood. It felt like the uncanny exhalation of a long-gone civilization.

'Isn't this the northern coast from where Ravan launched his attack on Kuber?' I stood on my toes to see further.

'Yes, queen,' Tillana agreed, his tension multiplying with each passing moment. I started walking towards the palanquin, much to his relief.

'How was Kuber as a king, Tillana? Was he nice to you? Was the kingdom content with him?' I reached out to touch the passing breeze, striving to stop it and request a document of the past. When Tillana suddenly dropped down to the ground, shivering near my feet, I jumped back by a few steps.

'Long live King Ravan. Kuber was a rogue.' Terror was evident on his face, but not conviction.

If Ravan was ever defeated in war, would he be labelled a rogue? Would people abhor all dimensions of his leadership? Would they effortlessly switch to worshipping the new king?

His obsession with invincibility had started making sense to me.

Ravan would never fade from the memories the way Kuber did – I promised to myself. Neither would he need to inscribe his emblem on animals or trees. No one could isolate his archives as forbidden. Thousands and millions of years after, Ravan would still be remembered for his scholarship and competence.

The swooshing winds ceased. The hidden tortoises raised their heads from the pool. My eyes locked with theirs as Tillana drew back the curtains of the palanquin.

*

The little Kuber was stripped of his crown now. He walked behind the army as a prisoner. The child impersonating Ravan walked up to a girl swinging away merrily. She charged ahead, her legs stretched forward. The boy sprang to the side to avoid being hit. The girl laughed aloud, leaving the 'Ravan' red-faced.

'Mandodari!' he shouted, reprimanding her. 'The greatest king of Lanka stands before you. Behave yourself. I will make you the queen of queens. This vast land with rich resources will be yours. You will own the land and the ocean, the sky and the underworld ...'

I covered my mouth with a cloth, lest my laughter alert them to my presence.

In Lanka, everyone knew the basics of Ayurveda, science and astrology. Those were the subjects taught in school. Most of the books had been authored by Ravan himself. His language was crisp and focused – no unnecessary embellishments. Teachers, students and even the novelists and poets were under strict instructions. 'Say exactly what you mean and make the message very clear. We don't want ambiguity. Don't rely on the reader's abilities to interpret. Too much freedom is misleading.'

The little Ravan was reminiscent of the real one. Standing before his mock-queen, he offered no polite invitation for togetherness, nor did he shower praises. If at all, he eulogized himself to impress her. His tempting proposal, however, fell flat.

'Step aside, idiot. You are fake,' she called out ruthlessly. 'My mother says there is no one like our king. Go back to your delusion and defeat the dull with that silly sword. No world beyond Lankesh!'

The boy and his group dispersed slowly, disheartened.

I frequently went back to the plains to spend time with the citizens. Sometimes I observed from a distance, seldom I would strike a conversation. This land called for a lot of unlearning and relearning. The genteel was loud and coarse – my sophistication stood out like a ridiculous, alien custom.

The rituals of the Asurs in Lanka were interesting. Every house had Ravan's handprints at its entrance. Commoners came across as hardworking and harsh. Expressions of warmth were as different as everything else. Their gentle touch left nail-scratches on my soft chin. They brought their smelly bodies too close.

I learnt to keep my reactions to myself. When people learnt that their queen had visited, they dropped to my feet and offered cold coconut water. Greeting an esteemed guest with plain water was considered impolite.

'Long live Queen Mandodari. No world beyond Lankesh!' The air got thick with their good wishes. Sometimes, I carried a pot to a village well and joined the other women in drawing water for their houses. They moved away immediately, indulging their queen. A few expressed an interest in the country of my birth and the family I was descended from. Complimentary counsel endorsed pastes and seeds that would unfailingly transform my pale skin into gleaming dark. An abundance of sunlight was recommended. 'Raw garlic shows instant results. Chew them uncooked and you'll be blessed with a mild fragrance. Your husband will stay glued to you,' one of them whispered into my ear. The children often joined as well with their playmates. When I brought out cans of sweets from my palanquin, they were overjoyed. Certain elders were anxious. What if the recipes of the new queen from overseas poisoned their children?

My sweets were poisoned indeed, with the dreams of a prosperous Lanka – unseen and unheard – grand in architecture, booming with resources, modern in technology and brimming with opportunities. The dreams of Lankesh.

*

On the other side of the sea, I grew up with my father, Mayasur, and brothers, Mayavi and Dundubhi, at a place called Mandore. Mayasur was a renowned architect, revered equally in Devlok, Martyalok and Patallok. Lores of the region insisted that one morning, daughterless Mayasur and his wife Hema had woken up to the crying of a baby. They rushed to the adjoining forest and discovered a little girl inside a well, wailing to be rescued. They named her Mandodari. My father neither accepted nor refuted any of the stories. He'd laugh when the locals reviewed the myth. As time passed, I too started feeling that the folklore woven around my birth were funny.

The forest surrounding Mandore was picturesque. Despite not being too far from the western desert, the soil was fertile. Several lakes blessed the vicinity. Extreme weather conditions generated rocks of varying tenacity and designs. Whenever I went for a walk, I brought back samples tied in the corner of my clothing and sat down at night to analyse their composition. I wanted to figure out if they could be artificially assembled to produce a larger mass.

I'd store the rocks in jars with my notes on how each material could be processed in its raw or amalgamated form. Father's instruments were whetted and polished. While grinding the rocks, they occasionally landed on me instead of their targets. Bandages became a much-needed accessory.

Meanwhile, Father had started talking to people about my marriage. Prospective families came to visit. They shrieked at my blisters, broken nails, bruised palms and the scars of deep wounds conferred by the knife-edged tools. 'It would be an honour to have the great Mayasur's daughter as the new bride.' They'd smile widely at Father, with promises to return soon with wedding gifts. Once they left, no one heard from them. His Letters never received any responses. I went back to the forest. The birds chirruped gladly when I touched the barks of trees.

The forest was my friend. I loved spending time in there alone. Engrossed in my research, I would forget when the overhead sun reached the horizon. Little Mayavi would come looking for me. He'd remind that my midday meal was untouched at home. Father would be sitting beside it, sharpening his cane to break it on my back. We would both run.

During one such expedition when I was busy digging out hardened soil, I felt something unusual. I was being watched.

The morning dew collected in the tree sockets fell on the dry leaves. The sound of droplets falling at regular intervals was nothing new. On this day, every time the dew fell, something moved, hiding behind the sound. The footsteps were subtle, but I was familiar with the terrain. The vibrations were consistent. It was not the fussy anklets of a woman. Rather, this could be a sturdy male. He refused to show up every time I turned.

I knelt to touch the base of the large tree in front. Invisible walls sprang up, setting an inner and outer boundary for the intruder. Neither would he inch closer to me, nor could he drift away. Trapped, he ran up and down the transparent tunnel and even climbed atop trees to escape the range of the walls.

*

I had been building a model town with clay and rock dust for several days. A thoroughly connected underground water reservoir was fitted with sensors. They opened the valves automatically and channelled the preserved rainwater whenever any parts of the land alerted of drought. Father was thrilled. He approved the plan immediately for the water-deprived patches in the west of the country. I wanted to accompany the team and supervise the work, but Father strictly refused. 'You shouldn't trouble yourself. The designs are self-explanatory. What if a good match comes up while you are away?'

I was disheartened.

My next experiment was an interconnected community-kitchen for the model town. Where to begin was the most difficult decision. I scrolled through the grass to find something – anything – that could spark motivation. Shuffling through the scrap scattered here and there exposed a fine collection of blue stones glittering on the grass. They had greyish lines running haphazardly over them. Such materials were not native to our land. They could have been dropped by birds nesting all around the world, or they could have been thrown on the seashores by the waves. Mandore was not visited by migratory birds, nor was it close to the sea. I didn't even have to dig them out. They were strewn about the ground, as if purposefully deposited by an indulgent traveller.

'Where are these from?' I asked directly, without waiting for a formal introduction. What came back was more than just a response. It was almost like a recital, emerging from the woods. 'South of this land' and 'across the sea' were some of the phrases I heard. The rest of my attention was consumed by the depth of the voice. Dusty surfaces of the forest shivered with delight, the cuckoos moaned and a few leaves slid off their stems to float gleefully in the air. His words echoed with charming pronunciations. It took a while for me to shake off the hypnotic influence.

'Who are you?' I asked, fondling the stones in my palm.

'I like to be called Lankesh. The king of Lanka,' he announced with a distinct accent.

'Lanka?' I repeated. 'So you are the king of a small island across the sea down south?'

His breath stiffened. The air grew warmer. I waited for his response. An offended voice is seldom fake.

'It doesn't matter how big is the land I rule,' his tone remained serious, musical and deep, 'as long as the rest of the universe is keen to be a part of that small island but is unable to do so.'

The *rest of the universe*, not the world. His choice of words was a compelling mix of arrogance and pride. I turned to take a look at this intriguing personality and stopped, shocked. There was no one.

Fine, then. I pretended to go back to my work. Dense smoke emerged from a few yards away, behind a huge peepal tree covered in creepers. A blast of violet fumes at first, eventually rising and flowing down to form the shape of a man. Tall and broad-chested, his body laden with ashes from many lands, a *rudraksh* girdled around his neck and arms. Flowing hair spread across his back. The serpents of the forest mistook him for Mahadev. They caressed his feet and climbed up his chest lovingly. He did not stop them. There was a slight dent on the right side of his head – did he collide against something in his childhood? A deep furrow between his eyebrows – he must be thinking a lot. His eyes were cold. Those were not the eyes that would seek material renunciation, and nature couldn't entice him either. Something was missing. The snakes soon realized that their presence was enjoyed, but the affection wasn't reciprocated. They crawled away.

'Why are you here?' I asked.

'Why are you here,' he threw the question back at me, his eyes fixed on the water-drainage designs embossed on the soil, 'where no one is ambitious? Everyone is born to eat, earn, wake up or die? Where your talent is exploited, and credit is not shared?'

A surreal hush fell over the forest. The last remark disturbed me, as much as I didn't want it to. Mandore-dwellers were laid-back but not incompetent. We valued peace over power. What would an outlander know? I decided not to honour him with indignation.

'Have I said something inappropriate?' My reticence had registered. He changed his tone from haughty to humble.

'What do you want from me?' I wanted him to leave me alone.

'Be my colleague,' he said, surprising me. 'Join a rising ruler in building a golden country to crown the earth.'

*Golden country. Crown the earth.* The man was quite an impressive show-off.

'The camouflage of Mahadev is intriguing. I am sure it is necessary,' I changed the topic. The lake behind the row of trees sparkled like a motionless mirror. The birds chirruped at regular intervals, buds bloomed, leaves fell, frogs croaked. But our guest was not gratified.

His lips spread out slightly to accommodate a brief smile.

'An attempt to impersonate the inspiration.' He stretched his hands out and looked upwards. The rudraksh dissolved into his skin; he shook the ashes off his body. Ornaments in thick gold designs fitted with rubies, emeralds, sapphires and pearls spiralled around his arms, waist and neck. Standing before me was an enormous figure with a muscular body flaunting many fresh and dry wounds. No wonder the cuts and blisters on my hands did not discourage him.

By the time he restored his full form, ten heads had sprouted from his broad shoulders! The faces of all the ten heads were identical. An Asur – my guess was confirmed. Unpredictable sorcery is the identity of the Asur. He represented the same clan as my father. Only one of his heads was real. The rest were mounted to confuse or terrify.

'Amorphous. Durable. Quirky. Magnificent.' I volunteered to break the silence.

'Are you talking about me?' the man was shocked by the strange mix of adjectives.

'No.' I smiled. 'I am describing the blue stones.' I showed him my hand, shocking Lankesh once again. He had not expected me to stick to the stones.

'The treasure on the other side of the ocean waits for you,' he subtly reiterated his offer, swallowing his disappointment. 'In the far east of Lanka, the tip of the mountains once opened to liberate the fire within. The molten earth was solidified quickly by the cool seawater, resulting in a blue mountain of silicon and cobalt spinel. After an earthquake, it submerged completely under the sea. When the sky is clear, it can be seen from the surface.' He paused as I rubbed my thumb over the shining dark blue.

When I looked up, he had crossed his hands over his chest, intently observing me. I was testing the strength of the stones by hitting them against the dry soil. His ten-headed form had received no reaction. To me, it didn't matter. Sorcerers, hermits, Gandharvas, Devas and Asurs came to meet my father regularly. I had learnt from them how magic operates.

'How long should I remain locked inside this circumference?' he asked, referring to the spell that I had cast around him.

Ah! I had totally forgotten. I got up hastily. A few warblers I had spotted in the forest that morning trilled from above. 'Why were you following me like some invisible thief?' I started uncasting the spell.

'I came looking for Mayasur and lost my way in the forest,' he admitted. 'I stopped at the model town to see its architect at work. Your father denied you the credit though he readily adopted your suggestions. Fathers are kind, artists are competitive.' Lankesh watched my face growing sullen. He had deliberately stepped upon a raw nerve once again.

'Father would be happy to oblige you, especially if you'd tell him about your dream for the golden kingdom,' I said softly, gently side-lining his offer to hire me. He noted it with a vicious chill in his eyes. I explained the map of the forest to help him locate Mayasur's home. He could rest there comfortably, enjoy good food and leave, hopefully after settling his contract with Father.

It wasn't too long after the stranger left that I heard scary screams. I stood up immediately. Mandore was a peaceful little place where everyone was engaged in some or the other form of art and architecture, selling a few of their wares and giving away the rest as gifts. I hadn't seen people raise their voices at each other. Expressing anger was beneath one's dignity.

I ran towards the village. The womenfolk caught me at the edge of the forest.

'What is happening?' I asked frantically. 'Where is Father?'

Amidst the gurgling of the women, I gathered that our premises had been raided. 'A gigantic man has arrived, asking for your hand in marriage.' An aunt pulled me towards her home to stop me from going to mine.

'He is holding Mayasur at swordpoint. Your father is ready to render all kinds of free services, but he only wants Mandodari!' said another.

Father's life was in danger because someone wanted his daughter! I wriggled to free myself from the women's clutches and rushed towards my home as fast as I could. There was a crowd in front of our gate. They tried to shoo me off. I pushed them away. Armed guards stood in position, their pointed spears capable of piercing bones and flesh. I had never seen anything like that; our doors never needed keepers. One of them spotted me and his eyes widened. He fell flat on the floor, his palms joined and extended forward, saying God knows what in a language best known to him. I walked past him and entered the house.

# 3

Our humble habitat, where colours, stones, sickles and bones of dead animals were once stacked neatly on the shelves, was now a heap of ruins. Someone seemed to have brought our belongings down to be packed. They were lying in broad sacks. Gigantic men were walking around, leaving dirty footprints on the sawdust-covered floor. My father's study was always illuminated and busy with some work in progress. Today, it was empty. No one had lit a lamp.

I walked faster to the corner where my father was being held hostage. Mayavi was seated at the entrance, terrified and crying. Dunduvi was consoling him and accusing me. The aggressive guards rushed forward, but maintained their distance. The shadows of dusk swayed like observant apparitions. The intense odour of the soldiers from Lanka greased the air. I could see them both from behind.

'I will marry her and take her with me. Whether by force or will,' the traveller threatened. His sword was wielded against Father's neck.

'Not till I am alive,' my father countered.

Lankesh was seeking a ransom, not romance. 'Why, Mayasur? You want her to stay around, and pass her accomplishments as yours!'

I could hear my father clenching his teeth in rage. 'I keep her away from the pride of talent. She works because it makes her happy, not because she has anything to prove. You are not an artist, you won't understand.'

Before they could discuss further, I walked ahead and stood between my father and Lankesh, the sword now lacing my neck too. My father tried to push me aside. I did not move.

'Run, Mandodari. He is Shaitaan, a sinner with some boons.' His laments must have reached the heavens. I held the blade of the sword and pushed it away from our necks, my palm oozing a river of blood.

'Why do you need me? Father is a veteran. He can transform your Lanka into the land of gold,' I said, not looking behind.

'You are way more talented. Your father is no match.' The voice still sounded like the chant of a pious devotee; his eyes were ruthless. 'Only the exploited knows the pain of oppression.'

*Exploited*! *Oppression*! What was he saying? I closed my eyes to assess the situation and agreed to go with the stranger, leaving him astounded and my father aghast. The inside of my throat dried. I struggled to stay calm and look indifferent. There were no signs of joy on the face of Lankesh either. His blood ran faster through his veins to gauge the scope of my decision. Behind me, Father was wasting his breath on pronouncing the perils of my alliance with Lankesh. He cried, wondering how his upbringing had gone so wrong that his daughter was desperate to abandon her kin for a horrifying, dubious assailant. He refused to acknowledge that we did not have a choice. I would be taken anyway, dead or alive. If I cooperated, the swords will be back in their sheaths with no collateral damage.

I walked forward with Lankesh showing the way, unheeding to my father's wails full of blames, curses and regrets. His relatives consoled him, advising that the adopted can never be one's own. They always strayed.

'If it isn't your blood, there is no real bond. No attachment can hold back the deceitful,' one of them said, nodding his head in sympathy.

Another quipped, 'Let her go. She was no more than a rejected piece that must run to the call of the first taker.' This opinion received great support.

'Throw out this immoral woman. No wonder she disappeared into the forest without informing anyone. God knows what she did!' Others agreed.

'Good riddance.' Everyone echoed.

*

People wear many masks throughout their lives. My brothers, birthed from Father, could do nothing to stop the sword hanging over his neck. But everything I had ever done was zestfully analysed to decipher how dishonest was the woman who wore a sinner's weapon as a matrimonial garland around her neck, so the naysayers could stay alive and blame her for treachery.

Why did I remember them today? Lankesh and I had spent years together, crafting our own stories of success. Why were these memories so fresh?

Ah! Sita was singing again. Her blunt lyrics about being separated from loved ones permeated through the gaps of the closed chamber, retelling my forgotten pains. I covered my ears with my hands. The music still came through. Sita was singing of farewell, seeking peace and justice for Jataayu – her friend, her brother and her confidant in the forest.

*'After being exiled from Ayodhya, we travelled for many days until we reached the Panchavati forest.*

*We didn't sleep on expensive upholstery any longer, but there was bliss. There was love. Ram was always with me. Lakshman was a guiding force, protecting us through sleepless nights. And there was Jatayu.'*

The song introduced an elderly eagle, as loving as a grandfather and as demanding as a child.

*'Before daybreak, he would sit beside Lakshman, forcing him to rest while he'd guard the little door of our hut. Why was such protection required, I didn't know. Over time, I realized it is futile to question love.'* Sita fondly recalled. *'By the time I got up, Jatayu would be dozing off with his head resting on Lakshman's shoulders. Lakshman would be wide awake, defiantly watching the world around him. I would come out and smile at him; Lakshman would smile back. Jatayu would sleep peacefully. We carried on with our morning chores as softly as possible, not to trouble the tired wings or disturb his sleep. He would wake up eventually and look around to see if anyone was watching him. Lakshman would make fun of him. Jatayu would retort that he never slept, that Lakshman was a liar! Ram would step in every time to restore peace.'*

I could visualize the old darling in the company of the three young people in the forest. Jatayu must have been tender, like all elderly are. He must be forgetting things, and remembering them later with embarrassment.

*'I washed him sometimes and ruffled his feathers with my hands so they dried quickly. Jatayu pampered my overt encroachment. He flew high up in the air, taking a round and coming back again with the dust of the world back on his body.'*

Sita's songs brought to Ashok Vatika many fragmented images from the forest they lived in. Lying on my bed in the silence of the night, I could see her past, hear her walking on the forest ground, envision her plucking fruits and feel my skin singed by the kind leaves that had touched her once. For days, Jatayu would disappear without leaving any clues. Sita would grow restless. Lakshman would start questioning the senility of Jatayu's old brain. Ram would look around in anticipation. When the wait became too long, he would shoot an arrow in a random direction. Within a few moments, Jatayu would be back, carrying the slender weapon in his mouth. Ram would smile at him and venture out without a question. Sita would hug him. Angry Lakshman would seek explanations for the irresponsible disappearance. Jatayu scolded with equal angst that he wasn't answerable to the foolish sons of great kings, infuriating Lakshman even more.

I wished there was more to the story of Sita and Jatayu.

Tears rolled down Sita's face. Seated before her, Trijata was also crying. Strange bonds develop when stories are told. We both felt that we knew Jatayu. The touch of his feathers was on our palms, too. I tiptoed into Ashok Vatika. Trijata was so engrossed, she didn't notice the queen approaching. I didn't want to be there; I couldn't stay away either.

*'Jatayu, like a guardian, warned me of the mysterious forces, the poisonous reptiles and thorny plants of the forest. I was usually cautious. Only once did I let my guard down when danger was lurking behind the shrubs.'* Sita was choking, but her prayers did not stop. *'Ram and Lakshman were away; I was alone.'*

Her voice dropped to a whisper. The tune was distinctly audible, and so was the deep pain anguishing her rhythm. Unknowingly, I clutched the corner of my clothing. From behind the bush I could see that Sita had clutched hers too.

*'When the sage appeared and asked for alms, I couldn't say no. I didn't think much. The old sage immediately transformed into the fierce Ravan. He pulled me by my hand and hurled me inside the Pushpak. The gigantic aircraft soared into the sky. I screamed, calling for Ram and Lakshman, pushing Ravan with all my might. The fox and the boars fled, fearing for their lives. Only one came forward, who was on sabbatical. Ram hadn't flung his arrow this time, but Jatayu flew in flapping his massive wings, hitting Ravan on his head and chest, pricking him all over with his beak and claws. Taken aback, the shaitaan almost lost his balance till he found his sword and ...'* Sita stopped abruptly. Her eyes were large, staring at nothing, taking time to process the eternal loss. Her silence hurt.

*'My brother, my friend ... the wing I caressed and washed with great care, tore apart. Jatayu held on the bottom of the Pushpak in shock, till he realized that this*

*was the end. In his eyes there was no fear, only sorrow. He released his claws from the Pushpak, staring at me as long as he could and disappeared into the clouds below.'* Sita's hands went up in the air, her palms joined together. Her eyes closed as she remembered her dear friend; her body was shaking with the agony of losing a limb of her own.

'Forgive me, forgive me, forgive me!' Sita cried out. Trijata wiped her own tears before trying to hold Sita in a warm embrace. I, the queen of Lanka, couldn't even gather myself to do so. Sita blamed herself, having sent Ram away for something absolutely unnecessary. She held herself responsible for bringing death upon Jatayu. She struck her forehead with her hand. 'Now I know, you beautiful soul, you never ever left us alone. You always kept an eye on us wherever you were, enjoying us looking for you, missing you, talking about you. Why did you come back? Why?'

The question would haunt Sita, perhaps for the rest of her life. Jatayu had gone too far away.

Left behind, she was the one who needed to forgive herself.

'Heal, Sita.' That was all I could utter before I turned to walk away, my insides numbed.

*

Pushpak, the bird-shaped flying chariot, was Ravan's pride. It had originally belonged to Kuber. When Lanka was usurped, the Pushpak came as a bonus. The golden aircraft could travel at the speed of mind. It looked incredibly real, with wings flapping so fast that its flight was impossible to capture with the naked eye. Unmindfully, after my bath that morning, I gathered flowers in a basket. The deity had to wait. I walked away from my chambers, leaving the palace temple behind, towards the rear end of the royal premises. Through the wide path paved with white stone and laced with colourful blooms on both sides, I crossed the sandstone armoury. Behind that stood the giant bird.

Glowing in the morning sun, the reflections in the glass eyes of the Pushpak made me wonder if it was really immune, or if it could feel everything but opted for voluntary silence like every other loyalist of Lankesh.

I touched its face, like Sita must have touched Jatayu's. No response.

The serene morning was filled with chirping birds all over the sky. The Pushpak was resigned. I stepped inside through the entrance in its belly. It stirred. I had to grab the walls to stop myself from falling. The bird-aircraft had seen a lot of bloodshed. It stayed as unaffected by death as it was by affection. I touched the floor to feel the skeleton of the bird from the inside. What if the Pushpak was the fossil of a beautiful bird that once lived, whose loyalty grew even after its death? Could Jatayu be transformed into something similar?

My head felt heavy. The narrow steps, like the cold lifeless ribs of the bird, took me to the terrace. I located the spot which Sita had mentioned, where Jatayu's blood had washed the railing. Quietly, I bowed before it and placed the flowers I had collected as offerings for oblation to the deceased.

So much had started here, so much the bird had kept to itself. This was the first time I had entered the Pushpak, so many years after I travelled from Mandore to Lanka. Each corner held a memory. That day, the bird had trembled as did my heart.

'The Pushpak is mischievous towards new masters,' Lankesh said.

'Or maybe this is its appreciation towards its owner's achievements,' I lashed out. Lankesh ignored my sarcasm.

I was not *hurled* into the Pushpak, I walked into it. One of Father's trusted attendants had followed us. I stopped for a while before the Pushpak, awestruck even in grief. Lankesh waited behind, following my eyes hovering around the giant vertebrate, all apprehensions subsiding temporarily. The aircraft demanded undivided attention. It intimidated with its elegance, and flattered its owner with polite courtesies. Strings of pearls adorned its neck, covering a beautiful dark-blue spot below the beak. It reminded me of *Neelkanth* Mahadev, the ascetic poison bearer.

My father's attendant tried to enter. The Pushpak lifted itself in the air, way above his reach but not beyond his sight. He threw his shawl upwards to girdle a knot around one of the hooks and climb up the cloth. The Pushpak kept moving, and he kept missing the clasp. Finally, exhausted, he gave up. He would go back to tell my father that I had been mesmerized by the imposter's property. From the window pierced on the belly of the Pushpak, I saw him leaving and wondered whether my father would disown me or try to forgive.

Was I really my father's loving daughter? Or was I an artist extraordinaire? Was my father pleased with my aptitude? Or did it embarrass him? Ravan had crawled inside my brain even before I had known him well.

This morning, I stood again on the shoulders of the bird. The golden kingdom shone back at me. Why did the disorderly forest from my childhood feel more precious?

Awful ruminations crossed my mind, dishing out delirious depictions of a gigantic bird, breathing and whistling for Kuber. After the great Lankan insurgence, a lot of the earlier history was destroyed. The Pushpak may have adapted to the ownership of Lankesh with meek and mute compliance, devoid of its erstwhile freedom to express or evaluate.

Suddenly the weather turned windy. A few drops of rain sloshed carelessly, forcing a full stop on the abstract visuals born out of idle squandering.

# 4

Below, the meadows and rivers, sal trees and buffaloes passed with speed. The woman with a basket on her head, the man in the field, the gossips at the stairs of the pond and a leopard approaching stealthily from behind an unsuspecting deer – I could see them all. With every passing moment, the Pushpak was taking me further away from the land, in the temples of which I had longed for a husband like Shankar. Every woman in Mandore grew up hearing the tales of Shankar's love for Parvati, fantasizing about such divine passion igniting their lives.

I could have been sitting motionless for hours – watching, remembering, reflecting. When

I turned to shift my legs, I was startled. Lankesh sat behind as if my musings were his too. There was a sandalwood *tilak* on his forehead, like my Shankar's. I glanced at him. Mahadev had sent across his replica in mockery of my prayers. Conscious and tired, I wondered what chivalry stopped Lankesh from forcing himself on me. It was difficult to comprehend what was going on inside his brain.

'The island is eager to meet you.' This wasn't the invader slapping his whims on others. It was the deep voice of the traveller with wonderful blue stones in his collection.

'So romantic is its invitation. It pulls people towards itself with chains if they aren't otherwise interested.' Though I wasn't looking at him, I could feel his jaws tightening again. The Pushpak registered a soft turbulence.

'The sword can fetch far more than the verses of a lover. I offer and prefer tangible rewards.' He stroked the edge of his sword and kept it aside. I did not enquire what pivotal life lessons made a handsome man sound so weird. 'I will wait forever till you come to terms with it,' he promised.

Lankesh sat patiently, perhaps counting his gains from my unquantifiable losses. Just when I had discounted him off as an inert piece of stone, he mumbled, 'Love makes a person weak. I can engage and exchange, but never love.'

'Really?' My voice made him turn. 'The greatest of the kings is scared of love!'

Lankesh did not defend his valour. He fielded facts in response to sarcasm. 'Those who loved you all your life couldn't retain you. They should have spent less time loving and more time training with arms. Love is the veil of the weak.'

This hurt. He was aware of it but acted as if he didn't notice.

'What am I supposed to do in your perfect life?' I uttered softly. 'Listen to great sermons on love and war?' He broke into laughter and immediately controlled himself, considering that my disconnect was not his entertainment.

'Well, I could be a tedious lover, but you would never find a bigger dreamer. For a woman of your talent, a dreamer with a sword is a mesmerizing match. My ambition, your execution. You will be the creator, and I, the custodian. A perfect partnership.' Now, he was rubbing me the wrong way. I could see the fleeting glint in his eyes as he waited for another sarcastic retaliation. I didn't bother to oblige him. He closed his eyes. 'The target is infinite prosperity. Our leadership vision needs the support of art and innovation.'

Lankesh glowed like a sacrificial fire, charged up to forego all distractions and focus on the selection of fuels to facilitate his soar. I couldn't trivialize his sincerity.

'I'm a theorist, creating models that are only pilot projects. No practical experience, no success record. Father would have brought alive the grandeur and richness you seek. I am too worthless for your big dream.' My concern was genuine.

'No, Mandodari.' Lankesh shook his head slowly. 'A veteran would be great, but he would complete the allotted task and move on. Lanka needs a fellow dreamer whose engagement is tireless and never-ending. Together we can create one success story, only one. And that one success story will be way bigger than the lifetime achievements of many veterans. You understand?' The crazy eyes in front may have sparked some madness in mine. The Pushpak groaned. 'Lanka is only a part of the collaboration. The mission is bigger and beyond,' he mentioned before getting up to walk away. Almost reflexively, I rose and followed him, waiting for clarifications but not asking for any. He stopped and smiled. 'Go figure it out, if you are intelligent enough. Else, wait for the time when I feel like telling you more.' He winked and took a few steps ahead. And he turned again. 'I will leave you with one last sermon on love and war. In your new life, never fall in love. Only care. Withdraw thereafter. It will be good for all.'

He walked away, tightly wrapping the thin shawl he was wearing, white coloured with a golden border, inside which every muscle of his body bulged and flattened. The sacred brahmin thread ran diagonally across his back. I looked away.

We stayed together, while maintaining a distance. Both of us were conscious of the time passing between us at its usual pace. I was disturbed. Lankesh appeared restless, constantly roasting some idea or the other in a vast oven lit behind his wrinkled forehead. Something told me this was to be our future: He'd keep throwing mysteries, the codes of which I might occasionally crack. I was to be the vessel into which he'd continuously pour his steaming aspirations.

That morning, I was sitting right at the edge. I could have jumped off; I could have fallen. Lankesh came by and saw me there, he wasn't alarmed. Calmly, he assumed a seat with his back against the wall. I was expecting this. No one could leave the Pushpak, either willingly or by accident, unless its master decreed it.

'It is powerful,' I exclaimed.

'And protective,' Lankesh responded. 'The Pushpak can keep secrets.' His eyes were mischievous.

'Do you need secrets?' I shrugged. 'I thought secrets are for lesser mortals fearful of being challenged, stopped or dismissed.'

'Secrets are for anyone who conspires to rise above an ordinary fate. And conspire you must.' Lankesh smiled. 'In our chase for an illustrious future, old learnings become redundant quickly. New paths are loaded with risks. Secrets are the swords to battle those risks.'

Had I not met Lankesh, I would not have believed that a single man could be a concoction of mesmerizing masculinity, inspiring philosophy, fantastic war skills, bottomless wisdom and unapologetic cruelty. My next question caught him off guard. 'What is the secret of the Pushpak? Where did you source this beauty from?'

Lankesh bristled, a wave of anger washing over his face. A vein on his forehead was rising and dropping. 'It was Kuber's. I defeated him in war … what!' he hissed. His irritation was evident, as was a cynical smile on my lips.

'Forcibly obtaining what isn't yours can be called gallantry by the victorious, but in basic language it's robbery.'

A few moments passed as Lankesh processed my cutting remark. 'When gold lies on a neglected path, the traveller doesn't become a robber for picking it up and putting it to good use. Returning it to the careless owner is foolishness.'

'The path was my freedom. You have invaded it,' I was despondent. I missed my house, my father, the people and forest of Mandore.

'I am talking about gold. Why are you after the path?' He remained indifferent to my sadness.

'The path is my identity; the gold is yours.' I was almost in tears.

Lankesh looked afar, without moving. 'Two disparate identities can create something spectacular, if both can let go of mundane comforts.'

'You don't speak like a king. You are only a vengeful warrior who extends the battle even after his opponent is defeated.' I accused. There was no doubt Lankesh was not done with Kuber. All his ventures, including me, were his secret cannons aimed at something I was yet to discover.

'Decisions might follow a protocol in the royal court, but in the king's brain, it is always personal.' He explained no further, neither did he get angry. I could not understand why he was being so lenient and patient.

The arrangements for our wedding had been made by then. Priests were ready to begin the rituals. They never got any instructions from Lankesh. The Pushpak stretched its terrace to make room for the event. When the priest chanted his mantras and poured *ghee*, the flames rose high, beyond where our eyes could reach. No gifts came my way, no threats. The Pushpak showed hills and waterfalls, creatures under the deep blue ocean and insects flapping their wings on treetops. I could also see the mountain of cobalt spinel far away. Ocean waves were frothing over it. Sunlight touched its surface, permeating the transparent water. The Pushpak, however, showed no signs of landing.

'Define your gold,' I awarded Lankesh the question he had awaited.

'Lanka! I want it to be the epitome of luxury, rendering every other beauty in the universe obsolete. Mandodari, my doubt is not whether you can share this vision. I know you can. The question is, would you commit to it?'

'But why?' I asked, surprised.

'Indra. Have you heard of him? It's good that you haven't.' His face was suddenly red with anger, hands fisted. 'A lecher of a man, good for nothing, neither brave nor intelligent, sits on the throne of Devlok to perform unforeseen stupidity. He comes with nonexistent credentials but is Vishnu's favourite,' he said in one breath. Fury flowed from his eyes. 'Mahadev knows I am way more capable than Indra can ever be. Someday I will smash the lech, tie Vishnu's hands and get the two to parade on my ground.' He stomped on the floor with his foot.

The Pushpak must be used to the tantrums of its owner. The king of a small island somewhere in the vast world claimed to be more capable than Indra and questioned Vishnu's integrity. Was this simple arrogance or chronic insanity?

'I will never bow before the worthless Indra,' he vented. 'To begin with, I want the spectacular country of Lanka to become the preferred destination for both Mortals and Immortals. But the Immortals will have no place here, except as slaves.'

I had been watching Lankesh with bated breath. His face was etched with untold pains, recomposed into an elegy of burning determination. When the deserving are deprived, they turn into saints. Or they become shaitaan. It was evident that Lankesh was not the former. I couldn't tell how close he was to the latter. As I immersed deep into my thoughts, I was startled by his hands over mine, his voice almost pleading without meaning to. 'If you are with me, Mandodari, I will show both Indra and Vishnu the power of the Mortals!'

His pulse was quickening with excitement and suspense. I didn't remove my hands from his. He wanted to attain the impossible. The impossible may not be attained, but who says that it should not be desired? I remembered Lankesh talking about oppression and exploitation. His words had started making sense to me. When Father had stopped me from building water-channels for the western deserts, I hadn't protested. But it churned and choked inside. Project after project that I could've taken on flew out of my hands. I always went back to the make-believe world of the forest and built model towns. Images of the missed projects floated before me like fluffy clouds, ridiculing me. Here I stood before the challenge of a lifetime. Lanka would have to be rebuilt. The designs would have to entice the Immortals, their access must be restricted. They would see, but not enter. The offer came from a king, who my father had called a sinner! Too many thoughts bombarded my head. I was swept away by the ferocity of his need.

Actually, who was I fooling? It was my need. Lankesh was proposing love – a different kind of love that wasn't between two individuals but between two professionals.

'Mortals wish to reach Devlok after they die. I want that myopic wish to modify,' Lankesh proclaimed. 'Natives of Lanka should be marked as elite and outstanding. Everyone from outside should want to forego everything, in order to win a brief stay in Lanka.'

The invitation was tempting. The project was prestigious. But I was apprehensive. He saw the ceaseless traces of hesitation on my face and slashed them with a final strike.

'The world knows how Mayasur works,' Lankesh whispered. 'They are yet to know what to expect from Mandodari. I am taking a risk, a calculated one, by employing fresh talent.' He waved his fingers menacingly at me. 'If you fail, I will be drained off along with you.' Stepping behind, he adjusted his shawl over his torso. 'The canvas is yours. The objective is clear. No one knows what you are going to paint. Go, establish yourself, prove your mettle.'

He breathed in deeply. A striking grin flashed across his lips. That night I was left alone, deep in thought. From another corner of the Pushpak, Lankesh kept the hours awake with robust strumming of his *veena*.

# 5

At dawn, the veena slowed down. The music turned pensive. The musician may have shared some of his burdens with the benign instrument. Eyes drooping and fingers running up and down the strings, Lankesh looked like a lost pilgrim determined to discover a hidden shrine submerged in the melodious notes. The veena translated the torments of its cherished companion into disciplined tunes. Power has its own set of insecurities. The tallest edifice standing on the deepest foundation requires the heftiest surveillance.

A carpet of marigold was spread on the terrace floor. A huge *kund* occupied the centre. I sat before it, folding my hands. The priests were dozing off; they jerked back to their senses. Brass and gold plates were tinted with holy symbols. The hanging bells started playing, nudged by the excited winds. Lankesh opened his eyes. The fire was lit without delay.

This was where we got married!

Standing on the terrace of the Pushpak after so many years, I remembered my wedding vows. A decision to stand in defence of the deserving and investigate whether cosmic prejudices can be pointed out, if not altered. I empathized with Lankesh. Defeat hits hard when one's opportunities to try are squandered. When talent brews in abundance yet recognition is denied. Our game was dangerous, the opposition was powerful. I couldn't decide which would be more destructive – encouraging Lankesh or discouraging him! My discouragement wouldn't stop him. However, if encouraged, the Brahmand would have ample time to witness our magnanimity before he was written off as shaitaan for daring to question the Immortals. As long as

Ravan had the blessings of Mahadev, nothing was sacrilegious.

I touched my heart with the right palm. It quivered like an arrow aspiring its first flight. Thrilling was the dream of a golden country – a proposition to depreciate Devlok with the development of Lanka.

I wanted to attempt the impossible.

*

Lankesh had planned our wedding night well in advance. The moon had agreed to remain in one position without compromising on the passing of time. It would light up our faces and keep our bodies bathed in its gentle rays. Only after we slept was it supposed to run and cover the distance.

'This is not right,' I said, looking at the helpless satellite bound by orders it couldn't decline. 'It may cause a myriad instabilities in nature, the consequences of which we aren't even aware of.'

'I can only ask the moon for favours; I can't hold back time,' he insisted. 'This night will never come back. Treat this as the moon's exceptional gift to a newlywed couple. May the protocols of the Immortals be shattered right from the first day of our togetherness!' He smirked. 'Indra would be furious.'

Lankesh continued telling me illustrative stories about Lanka – the subjects and rituals, the animals and township.

'What was the name given to you when you were born?' I asked, feeling conscious about sitting so close to the man who was now my husband.

'My father called me Dashagreeva,' he answered with a strange reluctance. 'Because I could singlehandedly perform the tasks of ten heads.'

'What about the ten heads?' About time that this was sorted. It was the night of our union!

'What do you think?' Lankesh tossed my question back to me.

I turned to take a good look at him. 'Ten heads are always in sync, one brain is manoeuvring the rest,' I stated my observation. 'Good for you,' I added. 'Otherwise, the conflicts of ten isolated minds would not leave any ground for Indra. Each Lankesh would have nine other Lankesh to fight with.'

In all the years of being married, I had seldom seen him laughing out so loudly. He took out the massive ruby–emerald neckpiece he always wore. He put it on me and pointed to a mirror in front. Now, he had one head and I had ten. It looked terrifying. I quickly lifted the heavy ornament pressing down on me and handed it back to its owner. Keeping it aside, he said, 'Mahadev named me Ravan. Meaning, the one with a distinct roar.'

Mahadev's blessing! It had to be special. 'Why Ravan? Why did you roar?'

'It is a very long story.' Lankesh blushed like a child caught in the act of mischief. 'I tried to lift the Kailash and Mahadev let it fall back on me, crushing my hands. The punishment yielded spectacular rewards, but let's save a few things for another day.'

'Would such a day ever come, when Ravan accepts an action as his naiveté?'

The way he looked made me chuckle. 'No wonder your father kept you away from his patrons. You are insensitively frank.'

If I was accused of *insensitive frankness*, then it warranted me the liberty to live up to it. 'Was Lanka your father's kingdom?' The simple question wiped the moonlight from his face.

'No,' he confessed grimly. 'It belonged to Kuber, my half-brother and the so-called god of wealth, an ally of Indra. I defeated him and chased him off the island.'

'Why?'

'Why do you need to know?' Lankesh was not keen to revisit this aspect of his past.

'The wife has full rights to her husband's discomforts as she is entitled to his comforts,' I insisted.

Lankesh looked at me, trying to gauge my intentions. He said as calmly as he could, 'Kuber mistook our dignity for our weakness. I had to ground him. No one can abuse my sister or malign my brothers again. Ravan will never again beg for respect—' he stopped abruptly.

Dethroning Kuber was his first attack on Indra's dominion. The win brought obedience from some parts of nature, much to the glory of Lankesh. 'Indra was appalled. Kuber's fall was a severe setback for the Immortals. I could almost hear them wriggling, cast out by their tattered pride,' he boasted. 'More, later.'

I nodded, quite certain that this *later* would never come.

*

On this plank we made love for the first time. Ravan was energetic, but an awkward hesitation held him back. He did not cross the threshold till I leaned on his arm and moved in closer. He fell upon me with his entire baggage. There was a lot to share. Not all of them could be explained with words, some did not even have expressions. I held him tenderly, helping him to release the bottled emotions. The touch softened his grip.

I ran the tips of my fingers over his nose. He arrested them, looked intensely at my eyes and let go. I guided him to explore the body instead of conquering it, encouraging him to go slow, feel more and do less. As I took over the reins of the night, he relaxed.

Despite not being told directly, I gathered that it was more than sibling rivalry between Kuber and Ravan. And it had gone too far for forgiveness. It began with Kuber, a privileged Gandharv beloved by the Immortals. Kuber reported to Indra. The deity preferred to distance himself from trivial ego tussles between half-brothers. Suppressing certain unforgettable biases which were never met with justice, Ravan's anger grew with time. He decided to outshine the celestial supremacy for good.

*

The next morning, the Pushpak landed on the plains of Lanka.

In Lanka, I first met Marich and Tillana. The latter was tasked to take care of me and follow my instructions. Marich was an uncle and dear friend of Ravan's. He welcomed me with great enthusiasm. An ascetic and well-wisher, Marich was quite vocal in expressing that Ravan had brought home a rare treasure. He came around on some mornings and watched intently as I made the arrangements to worship Shankar in a small corner of the massive palace.

Lankesh had a massive temple of his own, open to all. Its priest was Lankesh himself. The arrangements were grand, the offerings colossal. White flowers were spread like grass on the temple floor. Fragrant sticks burnt on the sides, emitting smoke like the mist of the Kailash. Water dropped tirelessly from a pot hanging above the huge Shivling. Visitors came from afar to witness Ravan's chants. He didn't simply worship, he performed the rituals. After generously sprinkling sandalwood and flowers, he lifted a huge lamp befitting his muscular arms and danced around Mahadev – taking tremendous leaps, circumambulating from one end of the temple to the other and whirling back, swaying the lamp before the deity, squatting on his toes, holding the lamp up above his head and standing up again, dancing and roaring *'har har Mahadev'*, with an army of devotees repeating after him.

At the other end of the compound, my offerings were modest. I bathed the deity and offered flowers that bloomed outside my window and fell from the branches in the morning. Tillana collected them in a small cane basket, I placed a pot of milk and prayed to the lord, wondering if my prayers would reach Shankar amid the ceremonious *damru* playing in the main temple premises. Whether Shankar heard my prayers or not, Marich never failed to attend it if he was in Lanka. Once done with my rituals, I bowed before the deity and bent down to seek blessings from Marich, before we proceeded to the main temple.

During one of those walks, he asked me, 'Mandodari, what do you think of Lanka?'

I stumbled, though there was no major obstacle on the way. 'I haven't seen much,' I said.

He nodded. 'The country awaits its queen. Own it, make it yours.'

I considered his words of no more importance than an elder relative trying to induct the new bride into her matrimonial duties. The fragrance of camphor and *mogra* from the temple had already started to engulf us. We parted at the gate of the temple. I walked up the stairs unmindfully, still adjusting to the elaborately embroidered clothes and heavy jewellery. They were part of my royal uniform. I took a turn to the left, where I was to stand with Lankesh. And I bumped into Meenakshi. The water from my pot spilled onto her. She looked up, cursing. I waited with an apology while she muttered a few words in her native tongue. A crew of girls swarmed in to help her.

I hadn't yet settled into my life in Lanka. The royal attendants were already divided into supporters and critics. Disapproval shone in the eyes of Meenakshi's assistants. They stayed away from me. The girls following me avoided Meenakshi. They were cordial with Vibhisan, the younger brother of Ravan. Vibhisan was neither intimidating like Lankesh, nor a snob like Meenakshi. It was easy to identify her as an arm of the royalty; every bit of her personality exuded her affluence. She was a fire bird, treating herself like a precious jewel, imposing on any arm and weighing it down. She would often walk into my mansion without permission, pick up utensils, open the wardrobes and leave with the jewellery of her choice when she felt she had indulged me enough with her presence. Things were returned later through Tillana, with pieces of gold coins added like rent. When I did not object or question, she lost her zeal and busied herself elsewhere.

Vibhisan, on the contrary, was a strict disciplinarian. He spoke softly and firmly, and only when he had to. Not a single word was wasted to silence those who ridiculed him for being odourless. Any ardent conversationalist would enjoy his company because he listened without interruption. I would never have guessed him to be the brother of Lankesh, had Tillana not told me. In Lanka, Ravan spent most of his time in the courtroom. Formal introductions with the family were for me to sort and settle.

What Marich had told me on the way to the temple circled back a few days later when I was summoned to Ravan's court. The stalwarts in there, gracing the tall seats, looked uncomfortable. Only Marich stood in the corner with a wide smile.

'Reorganizing Lanka is my dream project, Mandodari. I would like you to take charge,' Ravan pronounced, leaving his advisors unhappy. 'I want Lanka to be visible from afar – to be distinctly identified as an enigma. Submit your designs and budgets at the earliest so we can proceed with permissions and arrangements. Work must start before the beginning of the next lunar month.'

The courtiers cheered, hailing the king's decision as one of the best they had heard in many years. Lankesh had moved on to other things. I turned and walked away as the eyes of the courtiers scorched my skin.

'Why her?' wondered one. 'How does she qualify?'

'So many architects rejected to dump the responsibility on a woman?' judged another.

Their lips uttered not a single word to me. 'No world beyond Lankesh,' they cheered in unison.

# 6

My father used to say, 'The king's palace is only a reward, symbolic of the exuberance of the king and the kindness of the queen. Greater the success of the leaders, the bigger will be the spread of the palace, loftier its roof.'

For Ravan, though, *success* was the fruit of another plant. 'A wise leader plays with the perceptions of the people. The citizens should see what the king wants them to see. The subjects should never be allowed to undervalue their privileges,' he had said, sitting on the temple stairs, long back. The devotees had dispersed by then, after filling their baskets with the offerings of the day. 'Pride for the country doesn't come from shedding blood and sweat with crafting and farming. Patriotism emerges when the subjects feel attached to the property that isn't exactly theirs, yet they would protect the honorary ownership with their life,' he explained, as the attendants cleaned up the ivory floor, and hung his veena on the wall of black stone. 'When the art and architecture of Lanka generate admiration and envy from foreign visitors, the residents will want to own more, engage more and protect more. Bring it to them in parts, over time, rather than all at once.'

I looked out of the corner of my eye. Vibhisan sat motionless before the deity, absorbed in his meditation, untouched by the chaos of the temple workers.

'People worship power, loyalty follows splendour.' Lankesh advised. 'I will get the power, Mandodari, you create the splendour.' His muscles rose and fell in excitement. The ribs formed strange patterns on his chest and belly, not a drop of excess flesh anywhere. The peaks, plateaus and plains of Lanka were illustrated in that large, bare frame. A thin shawl left loosely on the shoulders covered his arms. He looked at me while speaking, but couldn't decipher the language of my eyes. Or perhaps, he didn't want to. He followed a no-distraction policy at work.

Lankesh was particularly conservative when it came to public displays of affection. No one had seen us sitting together hand in hand, one's head on another's shoulder, or anything else that lovers do. About the estate, however, he was crystal clear and never withdrawn. Impatience and enthusiasm often made him impolite.

'The sight of Lanka must reward the lech with a thousand deaths,' he murmured, remembering a recent attack he had launched. The Devraj had escaped, making a fool of his enemies on the battlefield.

On that sultry evening, I was walking hastily towards my chambers to complete some chores, thinking about all these and more. The sun had set, twilight taking over. I hadn't even prepared the earthen lamps. A pair of hands pulled me into the corner and, before I realized, I slipped into the garden behind, where the breeze was pleasant and fireflies raised a din.

'Are you a woman or a feather?' Voice dipped in desire, his fingers tickled upwards over my bare back.

With a deep breath I inhaled the rugged scent. 'Are you a king or a lover?'

Lankesh stopped rubbing his lips against my neck and looked up with a frown. He had a ridiculous aversion to being called a *lover*. I chuckled and put a hand behind his head, bringing his lips back to where they should be. Just before he resumed, I pushed him onto the grass and climbed atop him. Taken aback by the forced change of position, he tried to pin me back down on the ground. I disarmed his mighty grip with a swift elbow. Joining the thin fallen shoots from the ground quickly, I tied him up against the grass before lowering myself like a tigress pouncing on her captive prey. Who said splendour should be limited to art and architecture? He moaned aloud, forgetting everything else.

His tough body and rough fingertips always left bluish traces on my fair skin. Vibhisan's wife, the short and stout Sarama, teased me about them later. I still flaunted the love marks, having earned them from a sober husband who was miserly with romance.

*

In the eastern part of the kingdom, some of the official buildings were left half-done for years because Lankesh decided mid-way that they were not grand enough. Besides them, the gurukul demanded renovations. Ravan wanted even some residential complexes to be redeveloped. Right now, things were too predictable. Too typical. Too common. Too mediocre. Ravan was struggling to find the right adjective to appropriately express his displeasure with everything that had existed since the time of Kuber.

'Explain your politics,' I interrupted. He liked the question.

'Politics is all about citizens. The citizens do not belong to anyone,' he said. 'The subjects are not capable of love. They respond better to fear. They measure the greatness of the king in terms of their prosperity under him. The role of the leader is not only to maximize growth but also to let his people know from time to time how powerful he is. If the king is too nice, miscreants will provoke, and the foolish will betray.'

Thin light flickered from an earthen lamp. It lit up a small portion of the huge Shivling. The rest of the hall was shadowed. I had caught up with Lankesh at dusk, after he had played his veena for Mahadev. He seldom earned such intimate hours on a balmy evening, devoid of followers and visitors.

'How do you want your subjects to be?' I pinned the context.

Ravan turned with great pleasure, as if this was the question he wanted to be asked. 'The subjects.' He smiled and sighed. 'They only seek happiness. They are either with the establishment or against it. The challenge is to demolish those who are against. Concentrate on the loyalists and stop them from falling to the other side. The opposing ideologues should feel like outcasts.' He leaned towards me. 'This is the toughest politics. And this is the only politics.'

'Is there anyone in the country who is not with Ravan?' I frowned.

He nodded slowly. 'Yes, there are. They exist mysteriously.'

Like Kuber's tortoises. I wondered while unbraiding my hair, sitting a few steps away from him. 'What if the outcasts are not discouraged? How do you silence unsolicited opinion-makers? By killing them?'

Ravan took a long time, thinking deeply. 'That's one option. And that's an easy option. But ideally, the last option. The other way to do it is to let the hymns of the favourable side echo so loudly that the deceivers can't hear their own dirge. Eventually, unmindfully, they would start humming the popular tunes.'

I was observing the contours of the temple door. Labourers were scheduled to arrive the following night. The entrance wall would be studded with blue sapphires. One night was all we had to complete the embellishments. The next morning, the temple would be returned to the king for his worship. No sleep for anyone in the team.

Lankesh was an insomniac, though he had no role in the operations. I had begun ornamenting the country. With each installation of mine, his ideas magnified, which in turn stimulated bigger improvizations in my art. Fundamentally, however, Ravan's leadership was all about playing with minds. It came up frequently in our conversations on evenings like these.

'The subjects seek happiness ... you said. What do you mean by *happiness*?'

Ravan crawled forward and pulled me into his arms. Surprised, I slithered towards him over the ivory floor. My forehead bumped against his chest. The orderly hair was suddenly all over my back. It wasn't night yet. In the wild fragrance of his body lurked many odd schemes, as farsighted as they were forbidden. His hands came up to cup my face, his hoarse voice affectionate. 'How do you always ask the right questions?'

I smiled. 'Happiness,' I just uttered, leaving him in splits.

'Let me begin with a more important antonym.' His eyes shone on me. He took a while to breathe normally again. 'Peace. Lack of peace leads to *happiness*. A peaceful life is not what people should ever get. Keep them under great pressure. Distribute the prizes once in a while. Happiness comes in spurts. In order for people to be happy sometimes, they must feel discontent most of the time. A quiet, peaceful life has no zeal. People get bored. Keep them lost but involved, confused but expecting.'

I looked downwards again, deep in thought. Lankesh didn't speak either. Something was flying around here, but it wouldn't run into me. I would have to chase it. A gentle tap on my shoulder brought me back.

'Build monuments that dwarf others,' I was advised. 'Don't leave it up to them to decide what they should be proud of. Choices spoil people. Show extravagance while providing the minimum. The power of a leader should be visible everywhere, mocking the capabilities of ordinary individuals. Let them believe that slogging for abundance is happiness and obedience to the royalty will usher prosperity.'

*

Tillana was instructed to escort me across the country so I could begin my inspection. We spoke during those journeys sometimes, once we were sufficiently distanced from the palace.

'I was Kuber's slave, adopted later by the almighty Lankesh.' Tillana wasn't trying to flatter; he really meant it.

'How did Kuber look? As tall as Lankesh with an equally loud voice? Dark and tough?' Tillana took a long pause. Finally, he shook his head. 'Now I know why the usually nice Kuber was so furious with Ravan. You are right.'

What was right if my assumptions were wrong! Tillana's voice poured in. 'Kuber was nothing like

Ravan. He was plump and dwarf, with a huge belly. He was respectful towards their father, Rishi Viswasrav. But when he and his mother, Varavarnini, saw Ravan, they were furious. Ravan was a child then, this big.' Tillana indicated with his hand the height of the king in his early teens. 'He was trying to hide behind his mother, Kaikasi, too shy to meet his half-brother from another mother. But magnificence is seldom compromised by modesty. Ravan was radiant. Kuber grimaced. *Who allowed the beggars to step on the royal floors?* The Yaksha screamed unexpectedly at Mother Kaikasi and Sister Meenakshi.'

It happens – inferiority complex often undervalues excellence.

'His insolence drew Ravan out from behind the veil of his tearful mother,' Tillana continued. 'Young Ravan's anger amused Kuber, inspiring him to enhance his cruel digs, especially at the young girl. Meenakshi started crying. Ravan quickly sat her on his lap, wiping away her tears. He vowed revenge and led his mother and three siblings out.'

Ravan's love for his sister, Meenakshi, was touching. Nonetheless, it was also somewhat abnormal. Blind love can grossly entitle. It can create a smog inside the mind, polluting the clarity of a king's decisions. This was not something I could discuss with Tillana.

'What happened afterwards?' I probed instead.

'I followed them, queen,' he reiterated. 'And returned to the palace of Lanka only when Dashagreeva became Lankesh.'

Why, I didn't ask. It was evident that the slave had betrayed his master to help Ravan win over the kingdom. From being a slave to a salaried attendant, he had come a long way. When respect is compromised, a monstrous backlash surfaces. Ravan was not a monster, but a part of his personality was. Tillana's account of his past told me much more than his sword and roars could. He was easily offended by small things. Hurting his pride could prove deadly. He trusted no one outside his immediate family.

Wait, did Tillana mention three siblings? Who else was there other than Meenakshi and Vibhisan? Where was this third sibling?

I called for Marich.

# 7

'You have heard of Kumbhkarn,' Marich confirmed, as if the information was unimportant. 'He sleeps for six months and wakes up only for a day before going back to sleep for another six months.'

'Strange!' I was miffed with Ravan, Marich and everyone else. 'There's another person in the family, alive and breathing on the premises – and I get to know months after shifting to Lanka.'

He shook his head. 'Kumbhkarn is Ravan's greatest joy when he's awake, and his greatest shame when he's asleep. That's why people stay silent about him.' Marich showed me the gateway that led to the underworld, where Kumbhkarn slept in a soundproof apartment. Few trusted attendants were permitted to cross the gateway during the six months. If he were woken up before time, his life could be in danger.

'Why?' I erupted. There were too many *whys* within one. Why was the brother a shame for Ravan? Why was he sleeping in an underground apartment? Why his life was in danger? Why was he sleeping for six months? Marich divulged yet another story from the past, telling me a little more about my husband.

'All the three brothers had a keen interest in statesmanship,' he explained. 'Ravan wanted power, Kumbhkarn was in love with luxury and Vibhisan intended to learn. After they had observed severe penance, Brahma appeared before them. Vibhisan prayed for the vision to always walk the path of righteousness. Ravan wanted immortality.'

'Earthlings can't avail immortality,' I blurted out. Marich agreed.

'Ravan was told just that. He rephrased the boon he was asking for. He should not die in a battle with gods, reptiles, animals and suchlike.' Marich smiled, appreciating his nephew's wit. 'These two brothers, Ravan and Kumbhkarn, were unstoppable forces on earth. The Immortals were fearful of their growing power and absurd ambition. They conspired against them. When it was Kumbhkarn's turn to seek his blessing, Saraswati Devi sat on his tongue. He ended up asking for sleep … eternal sleep. Mortals couldn't be granted immortality, nor could they be given death. He received six months of sleep and one day of awakening.'

Ravan was not mad at the Immortals for nothing. He had enough reasons for resentment. Before I could move on, something else struck me. 'What had Kumbhkarn decided to ask for?'

Marich was pleasantly surprised. 'Ravan says you have the capacity to separate water from milk. Information cannot confuse you.'

In this land, appreciation didn't translate into gratitude. It was only a confirmation that one was aligned with what was expected of her. I smiled and waited to hear more.

'Ravan and Kumbhkarn wanted to expand their empire across the universe,' Marich said. 'Hence, Ravan desired invincibility and Kumbhkarn wanted ... Indralok!'

Indralok! Ah, I should have guessed. Vishwakarma is said to have crafted the magical city brick by brick, his architectural prowess blending with the magnificent illusion of Devraj himself. No two visitors to Indralok had the same experience. The greedy found riches there, the wise discovered richness. Many reported that Indra's realm was seductive and luxurious. A few also documented that Indralok patronized the fellowship of brilliant warriors and dedicated scholars. Indralok was a fantastic myth, a collection of questions for many, a conclusive answer to none.

Since Indralok was out of reach, Ravan launched Project Lanka to eclipse it! Things were getting alluring and unnerving. Father always said that history never forgives and history never forgets. It was meaningless for any of us to ponder over the possible consequences of this ambitious attempt. There was nothing to reconsider. The ship had sailed.

*

The day before Shivratri, the temple was decked with marigolds and jasmines. Waves in the middle of the ocean danced to the jingles of silver bells hung across the portico. A stream of earthen lamps meandered over the campus. Sarama was supervising the huge utensils gathered in the kiosk kitchen behind the temple. The entire morning had gone with both of us taking stock of the supplies and confusing the calculations every now and then. Devotees had turned up from near and far. Lanka was festive.

A few hours before dawn, we sat on the grass with our backs touching each other's. My head rested on Ravan's shoulder and his on mine. I stared at the northern sky. His eyes were fixed towards the south. He ran his fingers through my hair, fanned over his chest.

'Given a choice,' Ravan suddenly asked, 'would you like to go back to Mandore?'

'No.' I was taken aback. Why was he reminding me of the bygone days? Avoiding certain old tracks evades pain.

He shifted his shoulder a little, helping my head drop onto his lap. 'Why did you come with me, Mandodari?' he sounded serious, 'Why didn't you use your spell again and trap us within those invisible walls? It cannot be that the spell worked in the forest but not beyond.'

'Didn't you take too long to realize?' I was amused. The man had started getting comfortable with me. 'When we met in the forest, I knew I would have to go with you. I wish the parting was more cordial, though. You should not have held Father by the sword.'

'Objections remind me of the resistance of the Immortals.' Lankesh gritted his teeth. 'Mayasur, an established architect, wanted his daughter to remain at Mandore so that he could steal her ideas. That man called me a sinner.' He scowled. 'But how did you know?' Ravan raised a leg. Lazing over it, my head came upwards, closer to his.

'Shankar informed me.' I turned aside.

He took a few moments to absorb my response and pulled me up by the neck, making me sit straight before him. 'Explain!' he demanded.

'Last year, after I prayed to Shankar on the night of Shivratri, there was something like a premonition. A serene voice swept across the sky.' I glanced at the stars scattered in the Lankan space, bereft of clouds. 'I was told that an ardent follower of Mahadev would come to me. I should go with him. Being his anchor was the purpose of my life!'

Lankesh didn't ask if there was more to the premonition. He slipped his fingers through mine and dozed off on the grass-bed. Although his body was relaxed, his brain was still working. Dreams never slept.

Mahadev doted on this devotee, the voice had boasted. Lankesh was intelligent, magnificent, charming, tireless and self-made. No one else could present the enormous palette I required for my creative colours to blossom. Elated, I wondered why this gorgeous Asur needed an anchor at all.

Immense talent is overwhelming; it tends to forgo its obligations – I was briefed. My aspirations complimented the ambitions of the Asur. Our lives would be an explosion of discoveries.

Every arrangement seemed modelled for me. There was still a catch somewhere – what it was, I could not say. What if my anchoring failed to manoeuvre the inexhaustible energy of the ambitious? I felt a tingling sensation about this divine orchestration. The voice had advised me not to think about 'what if's. I was free to explore myself instead of controlling others. If the earth was ever in trouble, Mahadev would intervene as he always did. He would take over and release me!

I turned towards Lankesh. The night was dark. His face was tranquil. He had extended no apology for having harassed my father that day. Nor any guilt for forcing someone when he could have persuaded her. Bringing up the topic meant he had addressed it. Consider it a prudent peace-making or a mutual settlement on his terms.

*

By the time Kumbhkarn woke up again and I got to meet him, he was astounded by everything around him. He hadn't woken up in the same land where he slept. The giant man rubbed his eyes in disbelief, creating noises of glee and shock. Kumbhkarn was taller, broader and louder than any other Lankan. 'Huhhhhhhh!' he ran to the seashore and slowed down at his will, raising his hands up in the sky and shouting with joy. His ecstasy sent a few children crying, while the rest watched timidly from behind their windows. Everyone was up in action, attendants ran arranging for things, the ministers in the court had all their documents ready to be presented, the kitchen was active since two days before, the palace was decorated with special care and the temple bells rang with gusto. Even Tillana was nowhere to be seen, entrusted with special tasks by the king. The attendants carried fresh clothes for him to wear after his bath. Tensed and hungry, Kumbhkarn walked briskly, raising dust storms. Lankesh was informed; he came to greet his brother. As Kumbhkarn ate a roomful of food to meet his voracious appetite, Ravan sat down leisurely and told him about the recent developments.

'You got married when I was sleeping?' Kumbhkarn huffed.

'We needed it,' he was told somberly.

'Who is this *we* now? What is *it*? Your wife?' Kumbhkarn finished a huge jug of milk in one sip.

'Me and Lanka are *we*. *It* is the wedding.' Ravan was unwilling to entertain Kumbhkarn's jokes.

His brother laughed sitting inside his apartment. The earth felt the tremors above. 'Good to know that you need someone. I thought you were all by yourself.'

'I have been the unfortunate loner whose kin stays around but not together. A sister who is busy sharpening her nails. A brother who must sleep for six months and wake up for a day. Another stays awake as if he is sleeping—' he stopped abruptly, disappointment writ all over his face. Kumbhkarn's laughter turned into guilt, but it couldn't hold for too long. He switched quickly with childlike restlessness.

'Where is Meenakshi? Why didn't she come to meet me?' he asked.

'Must be somewhere, having fun in the great kingdom, consuming much and constructing little,' Ravan ranted.

'She is your headache,' Kumbhkarn laughed again, teasing Ravan. 'You have always been partial to her. Loved her more than us and let her be the way she is. Pampered her like a baby. If she was here now, your accusations would be replaced with a lullaby,' he poked Ravan.

'Really? Who shielded her when she broke the string of my veena?' Ravan shot back, only to invite a loud laughter from his huge-bellied sibling.

'Who else but me! I witnessed soon after how my angry brother, the mighty Dashanan, was reduced to rust when she lied forthrightly with tears in her eyes that she had never touched a vain instrument like the veena!'

'I didn't.' Ravan covered his face.

'You did.' Kumbhkarn slapped his back.

'Come to the court,' Ravan said, getting up for work.

'You proceed. I will follow only after meeting my sister-in-law,' he said stubbornly. Before the elder brother could say anything, they heard me from outside the door.

'I am here, I had been waiting to meet as well. May I enter?'

Startled, both men looked towards the entrance. Kumbhkarn sprang forward and joined his hands, bowing before me. 'What do I give you, sister?' He held my hand affectionately. 'What treasure would I have to felicitate the flawless?' I blushed. Kumbhkarn sat before me, wondering what to say, how to talk. Ravan left in broad steps with a smirk, but not before reminding that he expected both of us to join him at the earliest.

'Give me your company. That is the most precious thing one might have from you.' My words made him laugh so much that he had tears in his eyes. After a few pleasantries, he brought me a box covered in white cloth. A stunning pearl locket engraved with gold patterns sparkled inside it. He held it forward with deep respect. I accepted it with equal acclaim.

Did this belong to the family? Or was it looted from Kuber's *tijori,* carrying the last sighs of slaughtered souls? Wherever the necklace came from, Kumbhkarn had preserved it with care. I smiled in gratitude.

'Sister, will you take me around the country?' My brother-in-law stood up. 'I want to see my Lanka again, but this time I will witness your Lanka.'

Ravan was informed that we were going out. He must be fuming on his throne at the kind of liberties being taken under his nose. The very possibility made us chuckle. Kumbhkarn's smiles changed into ecstasy soon. He looked around like a newborn just out of the mother's womb, introduced to a gush of sunlight and many new prospects to discover. He stood dumbfounded on top of the pillars, on the path that he walked, shrieking at times, or just expressing delight.

In our refurnishing of Lanka, we wanted more than a mere replication of Indralok. Imaginations had no boundaries, and merits were unlimited. Parts of the country were encrusted in gold. Crystals were mounted on the top of the monuments, with their directions manually adjusted. When the sun fell on them, they demolished the darkness below the sea. The seashore was clean, the sand dazzled. Trees had transparent pebbles of the sea hanging from them, sparkling in the moonlight. Canals were dug in different parts of the country for irrigation water to reach far and wide, carrying the excess fertility from one part of the land to recharge the barren soil in another. Glass pathways were rivetted over the canals. People walked over them, watching the fish playing under their feet in the transparent water. Roofs of the houses were interlined with stones that could control the celestial giants, robbing their strengths and rendering them deficient. Vayu and Surya, Chandra and Varun – none was spared. The Immortals came begging for mercy. 'No disasters from the sun, the wind or the sea should touch Lanka. No drought, storm or flood,' Ravan imposed the condition. Once agreed, we brought down the stones from the roofs and buried them under my quarters for safe custody.

Natural calamities couldn't touch Lanka now; Lankesh was supreme. The Immortals were constrained by the might of the Mortals! The residents cheered, 'No world beyond Lankesh.'

Kumbhkarn gushed in appreciation, overwhelmed, 'This is unbelievable.' He jumped around, experiencing the carefully renovated land, called the *golden kingdom*.

Up went glass buildings that mirrored the view in front and stretched the frontiers of reality into an infinite, virtual geography. Lanka felt far bigger than a small island. For a few months, the subjects stayed engrossed with the palatial constructions. Before their excitement could die down, they were greeted with yet another restructuring.

On bright moonlit nights, Ravan would stand on the palace terrace. He'd instruct the moon to light up a direction of his choice. He watched the ensemble of edifices raising their heads at different parts of the land, enthralling the citizens within the island and raising discussions of envy in every place that wasn't Lanka. The complex constructions of the country were shining brighter than the galaxies in the sky. He looked up and laughed at some absent rival with mockery in his eyes.

The soldiers' camp was established on the tallest of the monuments. Coast guards were deployed on stupendous structures erected near the sea. From afar, they could spot the rival ships venturing towards Lanka. Mirrors from the towers would immediately turn towards them, casting blinding reflections to hinder their progress. In the meantime, from this end fighter ships would shoot into the sea. Smart enemies attempted to use submarines for underwater attacks. Mirages were set up to deflect them towards deeper waters. Whirlwinds lapped them into their folds, rendering the vehicles and their passengers untraceable.

We welcomed trade ships gracefully from countries in the east and the west. The economy of the country registered steady growth. Manufacturing and packaging industries boomed. Spices and cotton, rice and pearls were casketed and sealed with gold coins carrying the royal emblem. Trade partners from other countries were kept in lavish guest houses constructed in the middle of the land. They were given a friendly tour of the country till they left with promises to return soon. Rumour had it that citizens in other countries competed for a position in the trade ships to win an opportunity to visit Lanka.

Diplomatic relationships blossomed, enmity weakened. The king was wise enough to refrain from fighting against an unequal enemy. He preserved his energy for a battle which deserved his enmity. Indra was his target. Lankesh was ready to wait endlessly for an opportune time to strike.

'Train them, Mandodari, so they could be of more use to you,' Ravan inspired me to find more aides in the country. 'Be careful to not educate them too much,' he warned. 'People should specialize in their work, it will allow us to grow. Keep them busy. Practice leads to discoveries, but knowledge leads to thoughts, thoughts lead to conversations, conversations lead to doubts. Sheer waste of time. They do no good other than questioning the decisions of leadership. Never empower them with the faith that their thoughts hold. Discourage those. Channelize their patriotism so they prioritize the country over self. The subjects should be intermittently reminded of their limited capabilities, in comparison to the infinite powers of their king.'

I didn't have to do much to ensure that. In this part of the world, Ravan was revered and also feared. People were united, partly because of the competence of their king and partly because our preparations were always a few notches ahead of their thoughts.

*

Raising a kingdom is an addiction. It's not a job where one completes a set of tasks and washes their hands off. A keen eye is always focused on the results and aftereffects. The goals never end; they only expand. Initially, I was working hard to fulfil Ravan's vision. I didn't realize when everything related to the country had become my own. The construction of each new building, each modification in infrastructure, the modernization of each conservative system brought a plethora of learnings. New feats flapped their wings, urging me to experiment more. Success leads to bigger ambitions and greater achievements. Nothing else mattered. I was sunk in the glory of creation. Ravan was a politician, I was an artist. I made the world look beautiful, enhancing the quality of lives. Ravan observed the perceptions of the people. So far everything was picture-perfect.

# 8

Palpable changes were visible on the island. A sub-sect had emerged under self-designated monks. They patrolled the country thrice a day, singing anthems dedicated to Ravan. In the evenings, after the day's work was wrapped up, they performed roadshows imitating Ravan's dance before Mahadev in the royal temple. The performers and their audience chanted together, 'No world beyond Lankesh!' Their anthem extolled the omnipotence of the Maharathi, the revolutionary, the Mahaveer, who blessed his disciples with eternal protection. The men and women of Lanka had started offering flowers over my footprints.

'Why aren't you stopping them?' I was exasperated. A few earthen lamps in the corners of my chamber had gone out. I poured some oil and lit them back.

'Why should I?' Lankesh was surprised. 'Sit happily and enjoy the attention. It is hard-earned.' He yawned, laying in the middle of our enormous bed.

'You are deflecting.' I clasped the corner of the bed. 'This is not what you and I wanted.'

'All I wanted was to endorse a fresh narrative.' He passed a ravishing smile. Fire from the earthen lamps seemed to flicker across his forehead. 'Songs praising the Immortals have dominated for generations. The Mortals used to be scared of the gods. They went to great lengths to please them.'

'You think they are not scared anymore?' I interrupted. 'If Surya or Varun or Vayu decide not to enter the country, we will be doomed.'

Ravan laughed as loudly as he could. 'Can Surya or Varun or Vayu make themselves unavailable, Mandodari? Do you think so?' He sat back, relaxed, and laughed again. 'Life is all about never giving up. And the earth is full of life.' Ravan leaned forward and pulled me by my hand. I fell beside him on the bed. 'If light, water or air start getting scarce, the earthlings will find an alternative. Else, life will perish. Either way, in the absence of the devotees, the gods lose their importance. The Immortals can never withdraw.' He stooped to girdle my waist with his hand and kissed my forehead. 'Always catch the opponent by their weakness,' he whispered in my ear.

The 'opponent' was a tricky term. Not just the Immortals, Ravan's opponents were also his relatives, peers and and even those monks who called themselves his disciples. The creative explosion of Lanka fuelled some kind of occult magic, enabling the Asur monarch to exponentially expand his zone of control. He tented inside the brains of others – including those he had never met – making them do things as he desired.

'You have constructed critical structures under Ravan Raj to detect impending calamities, should the Immortals betray.' Fanatic eyes glistened over me. 'The anthems of the monks are documenting this narrative of a Mortal cornering the Immortals.' He untied a tassel that held some of my necklaces together.

'The narrative you sponsor also includes the tears of the women in the erotic corridors at the outskirts of the city.' My tone made him stop. 'Where each beauty gets to seduce you only once in their lifetime and are discarded thereafter to rot in celibacy!'

Lankesh distanced himself a little, frowning at me. 'Queen, there are certain things that don't warrant a discussion ...'

'So perversion can spread its wings without guilt?' I cut him short. 'At least set them free so they can have a life of their own!'

'Have you ever heard of the celestial nymphs Rambha and Urvashi being set free from Indralok? Every assembly has its protocols,' he tried to elaborate. 'Imagine the lech pleasuring himself with three Apsaras at a time ...'

'Lankesh! You are using Indra to justify your infidelity,' I exclaimed. 'I thought Indra is ordinary and you are exceptional! When did you start comparing yourself to him like an equal? Why are you replicating his follies?'

'You are right. What's the confusion? I am here to prove that whatever Indra does, I can do better. Each and every thing, including this.' The bedside lamp emitted the fragrance of dried pine and pumpkin, gifted by our trade allies. Lankesh tilted his head backwards with great contentment. 'If you are getting jealous, then you don't need to,' he assured.

I sat up, pushing him away. 'We will discuss my jealousy some other time.' I fumed, 'How is this fair, Lankesh? It is cruel. The women there have the right to a good life, to marry and have children if they so desire. Let them go.'

Ravan lowered on the side of the bed with his eyes closed. 'Go where? Have you thought about that?' The smoke from the lamp passed through his hair strands. 'The women used by the king are higher-ranked than anyone else in the country. Many of these girls entered the house by choice. From widows to prostitutes, virgins to transgenders – I have never discriminated. Everyone is welcome as long as they can hold the king's attention.'

'Could they?' My brief question made Lankesh open his eyes and look at me, confused.

'Hold the king's attention? Could you love any of them?' I sighed.

'Lankesh wouldn't love anyone. Love is a trap,' he repeated stubbornly and and went back to inhaling the fragrance. 'About the girls, they are happier there than they can be anywhere else. I have ensured greater luxury for them than Rambha and Urvashi at Indralok. Their doors have no guards, by the way, in case they would like to explore the outer world.' He laughed louder this time. The entire country laughed with him.

*

I didn't tell Kumbhkarn about all of this. I had some other update to burden him with. After a tour of Lanka, we were walking towards the court when I carefully broached the subject.

'Kumbhkarn, I need your help with something,' I said softly. This was sensitive.

'My help?' he was surprised.

'While inspecting the sites, I saw something. I have kept it to myself as I didn't know who to divulge this information to. Vibhisan is too forthright. Ravan is ...' I trailed off, almost talking to myself.

'Temperamental,' he completed the sentence. 'I've called you a sister. You're like Meenakshi to me. I'll do everything I can to help.'

'It's about Meenakshi,' I mumbled.

'I can understand.' He smiled warmly. 'She's the only sister of three brothers, sometimes more brattish than we would want her to be. Too pampered, and her whims are heavily indulged. She must have been impolite with you. Ignore her. We thought she'd be fine when she grew up. She never grew up.' He laughed at the joke. When I didn't join in, he sobered.

'What has she done now?'

I hesitated, looking at the ground. 'I have seen her with Vidyutjihv.'

'Who?' Kumbhkarn jumped and stood motionless in the middle of the path. His face was red with anger. 'With Vidyutjihv? Doing what?'

I kept silent, leaving little to the scope for imagination. Kumbhkarn thumped his head with the back of his hand.

'This woman has always been a pest. Atrocious, horrible. I will chop her to pieces!' he shouted. Alarmed, I pressed my fingers against his arm to calm him down. He understood the signal and stood in silence, trying to control his increased heartbeats. 'Where did you see her, and when?'

I stayed quiet again. How could I tell him that I had seen his sister making love with the much-married Danav, not once and not in one place! There was no garden, no forest left out by the philanderers, as long as they were far away from the king's palace. Ravan had not extended any barrier for his beloved sister. Onlookers had no courage to report this. Meenakshi was using everything to her advantage. The couple was often found chasing Kuber's tortoises in the forbidden land while falling into each other's arms. The Danavs were staunch enemies of the Rakshas, both being rival castes among the Asurs. Lankesh, a devout Rakshas, had his darling sister romancing a traitor!

'Did she see you?' Kumbhkarn asked with concern, cutting through my thoughts.

I nodded.

'What a reckless creep,' he scowled. 'Ravan is blind. Your words would sink into the deep sea like a punctured ship if Meenakshi is confronted. She will retaliate with a reverse story and set you up in the firing line. Your integrity would be doubted, relationships would sour,' he said as a matter of fact, just as I had feared.

Kumbhkarn walked slowly, I followed him in silence. As we reached the palace, we could see Ravan waiting outside the courtroom. 'Don't you worry. Leave this to me. You won't be involved, but Ravan will be informed,' he whispered, his state of mind hidden behind his assurances now. I felt sorry for Ravan, for whatever was to transpire from here on. Yet, I was relieved.

Kumbhkarn stayed engrossed in the courtroom riddles for the entire day, as Ravan wanted him to. He heard out the issues concerning the royalty with deep concentration and passed his judgements intermittently. The renovated topography of the country with the latest architectural and infrastructural modifications demanded amendments in regulations and policies. The study was going on in full swing. Kumbhkarn bent down on the designs spread on the floor, asking questions to check the engineering of the projects. He thoroughly debated with me on the angular placements of the mirrors and the canals.

In Lanka, obligatory fitness regimes had been established for every citizen. Training in military activities and Ayurveda were compulsory for all. Skills were to be updated every five years through a neatly monitored process that divided trainees into age slabs. During my fortnightly inspections, I stopped to interact with the residents. Pride shone in their eyes with a ferocious belongingness to this soil. The children were healthy and energetic. In Ravan's dreamland, everything and everyone was bigger than the obvious.

'Why are the centres of scientific experiments set up in different parts of the country? Shouldn't they be concentrated on a stretch of land? There would be some learning exchange between the stalwarts,' Kumbhkarn suggested.

I glanced at Lankesh. The centre for scientific experiments housed scientists with great knowledge and mysterious potentials. These were talented employees migrated from faraway lands. They brainstormed rigorously with Ravan himself. Only the king knew how he established contacts in secrecy and convinced them to leave their country forever without informing the leaders of their lands. I led the royal guards of Lanka in, smuggling them through discreet pathways. Every successful migration was a thrilling operation for all of us.

The scientists entered the country under the condition that they would never return to their homelands. Such talents were welcomed with a room full of jewels. They were put up in luxurious villas and supplied everything at the doorstep, from pets and books to skilled masseurs. The scientists were not permitted to cross the boundaries of the estates allocated to them. The invention centres occupied a large section in every villa.

These villas were built apart, but within a defined circumference enclosing the king's palace in the middle. Lankesh was personally invested in them. He learnt the language of each scientist. They would only speak with and report to Ravan. Their needs and progress were directly conveyed to the king. Separated by the language barriers, no one else had any kind of access to their work – not even me.

The scientists came with great interest and contributed significantly to advance the technology of the country. The fantastic fauna of Lanka, combined with Ravan's vast knowledge of the Ayurveda, resulted in the medical vision foaming out. Experiments were conducted to find instant cures for diseases. Miraculous new drugs were sent for testing. Based on my demands for the constructions, metals were mixed to create alloys that were stronger or weaker than the original. Exports multiplied, commanding higher prices than ever before.

However, in spite of the luxury of knowledge and remuneration, the scientists registered a gradual decline in their energies. Within a few months, they looked feeble with dark circles under their eyes. Their muscles disappeared, leaving behind a bare skeleton. They breathed heavily, looked lost, always sleepy – the most brilliant minds of the time were losing their lustre. Loss of memory was common. Perhaps it was the pressure of work or the poisonous residue of the experiments – who knows!

Lankesh nodded with a non-committal gaze at Kumbhkarn, agreeing that his brother's observation made good sense, and his proposition to bring the discovery centres together on one stretch of land would be seriously considered. I knew it would never happen. Learning exchange was not for Ravan; he was more comfortable with isolated facilities.

Kumbhkarn's waking hours were coming to an end. We walked him to his apartment, where dinner was being served. I promised that the next time, I would feed him the delicacies of Mandore from my kitchen. Sensing the brothers' need for privacy, I excused myself. On my way out, I found Meenakshi running down the stairs. She pushed me out of her way. As she kicked open the door, Ravan let out an indulgent laughter at his sister's incivility. I froze, my palms sweaty with tension.

Within moments, the earth was shaken by Meenakshi's wails and Ravan's howls. The attendants stopped in shock, unsure of what had gone wrong and who was expected to correct the situation. I dashed towards the source of the noise.

Inside, Meenakshi was in tears. Lankesh was calling out to Kumbhkarn, demanding more information. Kumbhkarn had dozed off again, his face peaceful and detached from all the commotion. When he didn't wake up, Ravan glared menacingly at Meenakshi. The desperate woman refused to understand how she had been breaching her own safety along with the security of the country. She should have known that her elder brother loved her too much to treat her reckless fling casually. No one had ever heard Meenakshi pleading before. She begged to be heard for once. Ravan didn't confront her; he just got up and disappeared, leaving the shaken sister crying bitterly behind.

The next morning came with a tornado. I was sitting alone, looking out into the vast world, thinking about the turn of events of the previous few hours. A loud bang on my door brought me out of my reverie. Meenakshi looked awful. Her eyes were puffy from hours of crying, her hair unkempt and clothes dishevelled. I rushed to hug her. She thrashed me so hard, I fell to the ground, hurting my ankles and elbows. She came almost flying at me to crush my chest under her feet. Perhaps as a reflex, I grabbed her feet just before they could land and pushed myself backward. She tumbled, hitting her head on the ground. Shocked by the unexpected counter, she launched at me again. This time, I packed a straight punch on her. Before she could absorb it, I threw her out of the door onto the royal path, where everyone saw her rolling down the corridor.

I was seething with anger – an emotion I hadn't known much about before. Even the strength my hands had just displayed was new to me. Was it something in the air of Lanka? Or did being Ravan's wife bestow certain defiance as a wedding gift? I didn't have the time to seek the answers. Standing before me, fallen in many ways, Meenakshi threatened me before a bustling audience rendered speechless. 'This day will have its repercussions, Mandodari. Wait and watch.' Before I could comprehend, she turned and fled, no one knew where.

Cuts and bruises were not new to me. But Meenakshi's razor-sharp nails had pierced my skin. Dark clots had formed all over my body from the poison she carried at her fingertips. My hands, back and waist were hurting. Sarama arrived with cold water, turmeric paste and a cotton cloth to dab the antiseptic over the wounds.

A few hours later Ravan returned, his sword stained with blood. Vidyutjihv had been killed. The military arm he was secretly planting in Lanka had been uprooted. Meenakshi was not seen again – in the palace or anywhere else in the kingdom. The best of the army generals searched everywhere. Lankesh shook with sadness, anger and frustration.

# 9

'No, Trijata, he never slept, as strange as it may sound,' Sita said fondly of Lakshman, her brother-in-law.

Kumbhkarn, my brother-in-law, barely stayed awake.

Was his seeking sleep from Brahma really Saraswati's conspiracy? Or did he simply render himself dormant to cut down on Ravan's madness? Kumbhkarn was as subtle as he was huge.

Another of Ram's brothers, Bharat, was ruling Ayodhya in his absence. Sita said, he never sat on the throne. The king's chair in Ayodhya was to be occupied by Ram's slippers till the eldest brother was back from exile. Bharat was close to Ram, though they were far away from each other. Vibhisan stayed in the palace with Ravan but was grossly aloof. There were too many eerie contrasts to pass off as casual coincidence.

Ram Rajya and Ravan Raj were two obstinate parallels on adjacent tracks that could never meet. The latter was blatantly authoritarian, the former believed in unconditional democracy.

Trijata was bemused. 'Lakshman never slept! How can a person survive without sleeping? I've heard snakes sleep with their eyes wide open ...'

'Lakshman is devoted to his brother with every single fibre of his being,' Sita recalled. 'To make himself available at any time, he does not allow sleep to fleece his hours.'

I could not tell much about Vibhisan, but Kumbhkarn seemed as selfless as Lakshman. Both were sincere well-wishers of their elder brothers. Lakshman served by making himself available, and Kumbhkarn brought succour by ridding himself.

Two bushy rabbits bounced by. One of them broke the carrots to feed itself and its companion. The other one was busy digging a hole in the ground. Sita was watching them. Trijata placed her head on Sita's lap.

'What are you thinking?'

Sita gently caressed her hair. 'I am wondering what they are doing now. What must he be thinking about me? In spite of his unflinching attention, I had failed him.' A few leaves from the shimshapa tree landed upon her. She didn't pull them out of her hair.

'Why do you say that?' asked Trijata softly.

'It is a long story.' A drop of tear trickled down Sita's face. 'I had sensed that presence around me long before the brothers did.' She paused, still uncomfortable with the feeling. 'When I roamed in the forest, collecting fruits or filling water from the lake or simply walking beside Ram, I knew there was someone else with us. A fleeting presence – you know there is something but can't prove it. I made the first mistake by ignoring it. Signs of disasters must be recognized early.'

Trijata's eyes had widened with anticipation. I was equally attentive. The memories stung hard. Sita's descriptions were too similar to how I felt when Lankesh appeared in Mandore.

'What was it?' Trijata opened a knot at the edge of her clothes, releasing a fistful of bright blue sand. She poured it on top of her bun. The blue streaked unevenly between her midnight-black curls, greased with a generous dose of oil. She rubbed the leftover sand on the back of her neck.

'Not *it*, she. She caused me trouble. She'd break the pot I would carry to collect water. She'd pour poisonous juices onto the fruits I plucked with great difficulty. She'd throw dirt and muck on the washed clothes we would hang up to dry. When I walked, something would pass at great speed, throwing me aside with such force that I fell head-on, hurting myself. She also scratched me sometimes. See.'

Sita pointed at her right shoulder. She had black patches there, similar to those on my body. Surpnakha's nails! Trijata stole a glance at me. I gestured for her to make Sita talk more.

'How could you ignore the obvious signals hanging over your head?' Trijata was appalled, as much as I was. We both knew Meenakshi's attacks like the back of our hands.

'The attacks were only directed at me. She did not like me, whatever be her reason,' Sita said innocently. 'The Panchavati forest was home to a variety of life – some marvellous and the rest crude. I cannot expect unrestrained friendship from everything that breeds in the forest. In Ram Rajya, every life form will have equal rights to exist, with due dignity and freedom.'

Sita always converged to this – her Ram Rajya. The concept seemed so spotless and impressive that it sounded practically arduous! Like Ravan Raj, Ram Rajya also spoke of dissolving the disparity between the Mortals and the Immortals. Acceptance was their way, rejection ours. Ram Rajya believed in the supremacy of celestials. Ravan Raj considered such devotion as a complete lack of self-esteem.

'What happened after that?' Trijata asked.

'One of those days, she suddenly came

home. She was standing outside our little hut. I immediately recognized who she was, though I hadn't seen her before. As dark-complexioned as Ram, her hair swept behind like a wild river. I threaded together colourful stones from the forest to adorn my neck and the arms. She was wearing some of those as anklets. She had split open another one. The ends of the thread were held between her fingers, and she whirled the stones around. Any moment a stone could come out of the loose thread and knock someone down. When she had stolen them, I didn't know. This time she hadn't come for me. She demanded … Ram.'

'Ram?' Trijata couldn't hold back her shriek.

'Yes, she wanted to marry him,' she repeated. 'Ram said that he was happy with me and would not marry again. So she turned towards Lakshman and asked for him. Lakshman declined, too.'

Sita's veil fell off. She wiped the back of her sweating neck. While other countries in this part of the world were experiencing spring, it was scorching summer in Lanka by the benevolence of the sun god. Sita was tanned, as was I.

'She appeared to have been raised in affluence, treating me like an impoverished inferior,' Sita said. 'I think her attitude towards Lakshman was no different. The marriage proposal she made to him was a ploy to get closer to Ram. She was youthful with a bold fashion sense.' Sita pulled the veil back over her head. She was also veiling Meenakshi's advances behind the elegance of her vocabulary. Meenakshi fashioned herself to tantalize her audience openly, discerning for male attention with the way she stood, curved, bent, showed or covered.

'She wanted a man desperately. When both the brothers turned her down, she took it as a rejection of her beauty.'

Why did their 'no' feel personal? Ram and Lakshman's refusal had nothing to do with Meenakshi. What attracted her to the wrong men over and over again? Earlier, it was an enemy of the kingdom. After he was killed, she mourned, fought and threatened, but wasted no time in trying out another pair of boys who were not interested!

'Eyes suddenly red, face contorted with anger, mouth full of abuses and sword-like nails pointed at me, she charged forward,' Sita recollected. 'Before I could react, Lakshman jumped in, guarding me with an open sword in his hand. She stopped abruptly, adjusting to the sudden change. Her mouth was still spewing countless insults about my parentage, upbringing, marriage and conjugal relationship. She somersaulted upwards to cross Lakshman from above his head and land before me. Within the fleeting moment, Lakshman raised his sword and brought her down with a loud cry that terrified the woods. Writhing in pain, she screamed with her mouth open, the front of her nose slashed.'

Why did Meenakshi always fall for married men? Was it really the charisma of the individuals, or did she just want to displace the women in their lives? Why did a glamorous princess want to be a wild seductress, that too for men who either used her or were not into her? Growing up pampered and in luxury, where her wishes were her brothers' commands, she had for the first time faced extreme resistance – not once but twice, in quick succession. She was at the age of desire when she sought to love and feel it reciprocated. Alas! Bitterness and snobbery could kill, but those were not the language of love.

'She threatened us with severe tragedy. Pulling out a piece of cloth, she bandaged her nose. We could see only her eyes. They were frightening.' Sita ran her fingers over the dark bruises on her skin. I touched mine. The blood clots had faded but the burn marks were there to stay.

'Lakshman stormed forward angrily. This time, she moved eastwards, as if the ground was slippery. When Lakshman moved east, she quickly changed directions to the west before he could reach her. She circled around us at great speed, scratching me more. It was difficult for us to keep track of her. She vowed to see the day when I would rot in loneliness, separated from Ram. Her chilling curses echoed in the air long after she was gone.'

*

Sitting in a corridor of the central temple, Lankesh was playing his veena. The island was peaceful. Not a bird chirped, lest it meddle with the divine melody. From a few yards away, with my feet dipped in the pool behind the temple, I could see him through a mesh of leaves swaying to his tunes. The palace dwellers were prohibited from visiting this section of the garden. Trees were taller here, and the pool more serene. Tillana had forewarned that the place was haunted by spectres, the holes in the trees were full of poisonous snakes, and the deceptive water was home to hungry crocodiles. The pool was connected to the sea. The water current had notoriously pulled in a few cleaners who had dared to step into it.

Lankesh took refuge in his veena whenever he felt deeply conflicted and needed to talk to himself. He had been terribly disoriented lately. Every day he came to my chambers, hoping I would have something to tell him about Meenakshi. Something I might have got my hands on. Truth be told, I did not want the girl to return. But the claws of responsibility are tight.

If the girl was not in any part of Lanka, then she must have crossed the ocean. We did not know which direction she could have chosen. How she managed to get through the water was another mystery. The nails were Meenakshi's strongest defence. Was it possible that she had cocooned herself inside a shell made of her nails and set afloat upon the ocean? When Vidyutjihv was killed, the Lankan army had traced pearl-shell-like structures with high calcium content in the pools of the forbidden lands. Disastrous arms had been hidden inside them. I touched one and my fingers oozed blood. Without a doubt, they were made of Meenakshi's nails, their ability to float was her sorcery. This arrangement would also help her escape the surveillance of the Lankan coastguards. I did not burden Lankesh with my assumptions. He never said anything, only looked terribly tense.

'Why don't you plead with her to return? Call her back,' I said one night, when he was turning sides sleeplessly. He didn't answer, just stared at the ceiling. I placed a hand on his chest, where the heart had stiffened like a stone. 'Try once. Say it aloud. Let the word of mouth reach her, wherever she is. If I were in your place, I would have cried and begged for forgiveness and done everything I could to convince her how much I loved her until she agreed to tow along.'

Lankesh pushed aside my hand with immense disappointment and walked away from the bed. Putting on the huge necklace which multiplied one head by ten and wrapping a shawl around his large torso, he left in the middle of the night. I sat helplessly. Indeed, I had asked for too much. The strongest man ever was advised to shed tears and feel lighter in his heart! I had expected the bravest man in the world to seek forgiveness from someone younger! He stood alone and distant, the ten mighty heads hiding the wily moon behind them. Ravan had started believing that the ten heads on his shoulder were real, and that everyone else with only one head was deficient. Many sighs spiralled upwards.

Our conversations about the country were hurried and incomplete nowadays. I was worried.

Ravan was a king first, a brother later. For a leader, even feelings were to be prioritized. *Raj-dharma* should be over everything else. Things couldn't continue the way they were going.

The man I had married was restless, unstoppable. I was law-abiding. His approach was direct, like the arguments of a deft diplomat who knew not just the laws of the country but also those of nature and the celestial world. He knew them so well that he was aware of the loopholes too. Lankesh was extravagant, while I was frugal. There was an air of overflowing surplus around him. Lots of wealth, lots of wisdom, lots of anger, lots of need, lots of arrogance, lots of women.

The country was rich. No one slept unfed. Ravan himself gave out doctrines on the science of Ayurveda every morning. He inspired his people to heal from injuries at the earliest, preferably through self-treatment so they could resume contributing to the royal treasury. Tillana went from house to house to check whether the health standards were being maintained.

Our industries were raising their heads to manufacture on a large scale. New products were being experimented on and approved at the centres of science. Specialized equipments were crafted to enhance outputs.

The wealth in the country came from a variety of sources, including the sea surrounding the land from all sides and shallow forests interspersed between populated cities and busy villages. Citizens were dutifully engaged in the expansion of the existing wealth. However, talent was kept in check. Ravan encouraged the professional growth of his subjects as long as it remained within the lower and upper limits he had estimated for various categories. I kept a strict eye on the balance sheet. Lankesh focused on the units that returned voluminous profits. Larger investments were sanctioned for them. Through heated debates, I forced him to allocate a reasonable budget for the growing businesses.

Art flourished on the island. Every home had murals on the outer walls. Colourful paintings and exotic furniture welcomed the guests inside. Tasteful sculptures adorned their backyards.

Meenakshi's betrayal had dismayed Ravan. The mighty one, who was ready to fight the Immortals, was shaken by the wrath of a little sister he had raised carefully in his arms. His worship rituals in the central temple had become more fervent. Visitors from all over the country who came to the palace temple for Mahadev fell before Ravan instead, tossing holy flowers and sprinkling cold water at him as he danced around the portico, performing his own *taandav*. Solace was nowhere to be found, nor was Meenakshi.

This morning, when he was immersed in his veena, the blood in his veins raced and contracted with the crests and troughs of the musical notes. A loud splash distracted his fingers from the lyrical strings. Shocked by the miscreant's impudence, he looked around. The birds on the branches above raised a ruckus. Eyes narrowed, looking through the dense thickets, Lankesh spotted me inside the pool. Quickly abandoning his instrument, he dashed forward. Halfway through, he found me slipping deep into the water, swept by its currents. A fierce growl rose from his chest, bringing everything around him to a standstill. He swore to jeopardize everything in the cosmos if his queen was endangered! The leaves stopped moving, the bees stayed put and the buds postponed their blooming. They prayed for me to get back to the land, alive and in one piece.

Without thinking twice, Lankesh dove into the water, pushing his way through in panic. Before long, his right hand was wrapped in a mesh of sea weeds, and he was dragged downwards. He prepared to fight some intrepid sea monster, but each time he made an effort, the rope of weeds wrapped tighter. Confused and startled, he was about to launch an attack when he turned to the east. I was floating there, holding the other end of the sea weeds that had hurled him to the bottom of the pool. Relieved, he noticed everything now. There were sea creatures all around us, vicious but distanced, trapped outside the invisible walls of a transparent tunnel. Astonished, he tried to grasp the weeds and pull me towards himself. I slipped away.

A soft smile returned to the hairy cheeks and anxious eyes. *What?* He gestured with a hand, his lips tight shut. Long, wet hair clung on to his hulking chest. I swam ahead, with him in tow. Surprises were meant to be intense and unpredictable.

We swiftly moved along with the water current, heading towards the cobalt mountain located in the middle of the sea. Thin pipes meandered vertically at the base. We climbed them to stand between enormous rods. A press on the left rod opened a stony pedestal in the belly of the mountain. We stepped in, and I pushed the right rod with all my might. The stony pedestal now shifted us upwards. All our interface with the sea was sealed off, and the pipes started pumping out water. A rocky slab was removed to expose a small hole. We crawled inside to enter the edifice. A flight of steps led us to the bottom of the chasm, where the waves were gurgling again at the bottom of the stairs.

Before us lay a bare cylindrical structure open on both ends. It slanted obtusely to fit itself half inside the mountain and rest hanging into the sea. I pulled Ravan inside the cylinder. Thick walls curved around us, our feet never touching the bottom. We were left floating in the sea-water with only our heads above the surface. The magnetic fields established in the vestibules prevented us from sinking. A lamp flickered high above.

'What is this? Where are we?' Ravan asked, distressed. 'Why have you made this?'

I pushed him against the tall wall. Before he realized, thick iron chains girded his neck and waist. He twisted with all his strength. The locks showed no mercy.

'Mandodari!' Ravan looked at me, shocked.

I glided closer to my captive, one hand on his neck and the other on his back. My legs wrapped around his waist. 'This is, by far, an architect queen's most romantic offering to the greatest of kings!'

Lankesh frowned heavily, eager to end the drama inside this hellhole.

'This is the underwater structure that will one day imprison Indra!'

*

Ravan stared at me blankly as the waves lashed against the sea, trickling through the silence. I removed the shackles from his body one by one. He remained motionless. Slowly, his eyes turned red with tears.

'Do you see that vault on the stairs, Lankesh?' I pointed upwards. 'Once opened, the water won't remain as civil as it is right now. Sea creatures would enter unbarred, stripping the water of its stillness and the prisoner of his sanity.'

Ravan leapt forward to hug me with the zeal of a pauper who had just been given a gold coin. He kissed my lips, neck and shoulders. 'Do you truly believe that one day I will dethrone Indra and drag him down as a prisoner of Lanka?' he whispered.

'Of course I do,' I said sincerely. 'Devraj Indra will one day be hauled inside and tied to this wall with iron chains. He will have to chant with the masses, *No world beyond Lankesh*!'

Ravan pressed himself against me, his fingers stroking my back and his feet caressing my thighs. He laughed, cried and loved as if he didn't have anything else to ask for. I could feel the energy bubbling inside his body, pledging to grace this edifice with its celestial occupant very soon. The waves grew tumultuous, frothing in from all sides. The snakes and sea anemones watched us from afar. The rope of weeds circled around our waist as we made love. Our heads, pleasured by the ferocious dream, floated like paper boats in the sparkling black waters. The fidgety reflection of the faintly lit lamp painted iridescent webs on the jittery water.

# 10

Soon after, I conceived.

Lankesh was overjoyed. For a change, even Vibhisan seemed excited. 'Lankeshwari, your child will sit on my shoulders and travel to every corner of the country. I will show him his mother's magic everywhere,' he declared, teasing me with a new moniker. Finally, a rare compliment from someone who behaved as if Lanka had not changed, Meenakshi had not gone missing and Ravan was not distressed! It was good to see that he stayed abreast of things.

A few days later, as I finished worshipping Shankar, I turned to find Marich holding a basket of freshly plucked fruits. 'May the child be as creative as the mother and as brilliant as the father,' he blessed me and presented a pair of small gold bangles. 'May the gold in his hands multiply forever.'

I extended the bangles back towards him. 'Why now? Give them to the child yourself, what's the hurry?'

He shook his head. 'No, queen, you must keep them safe. I will be away when your child comes to earth.'

'Away! Where?' I was surprised. Did Ravan know?

'I am retiring to the forest.' He smiled gracefully. 'I have come to say goodbye.'

'What? Why?' I clasped his hands.

He gently placed his hand on mine. 'It is an inner call, queen. Every day, I feel I am nearing the phase when the purpose of my life will be accomplished. I must detach.'

The renunciation of Marich was difficult to swallow. He sounded firm, but irrational. Sarama, my constant companion since my pregnancy was announced, joined us. Tillana followed, a few steps behind. The conversation came to an end as we proceeded towards the central temple. That was the last time I saw Marich.

*

Trijata reported that Ram Rajya aimed to harness the unlimited potential of its subjects. Under Ram Rajya, everyone would be the king. The state head would be no more than a people's correspondent to ensure that dreams were unbounded, questions were plentiful, answers were wise and intelligence was encouraged. Every individual would be empowered enough to participate in decision-making along with the king. They would enjoy the rights to disagree with the king and enforce suitable course correction by popular consent. The king will abide by their choice, even if he is against it personally, unless he convinces his subjects with appropriate alternatives!

'Absurd.' I clutched the corner of my bed. 'The commoners cannot handle such liberties.'

'Be prepared for Ram Rajya to be a grand failure, my beloved!' the voice floated in from Ashok Vatika. Startled, we looked at each other.

'The head of Ram will be crushed under my feet. His rajya will be overrun with wild fruitless trees, whose shadows will form pus-filled blisters on the skin of the resting travellers.' We heard Lankesh nearing Sita when we ran down the balcony. Sita's songs were faintly audible. She was lost in the time she spent with Ram. Her song described the morning sunlight illuminating some parts of the forest, while the rest was left in the dark under the canopy of interlocked branches.

'People would be worse than hooligans, their demands towering over the Kailash. But the royalty will be approachable, and subjects will be powerful,' he mocked and laughed. We dashed through the portico, with Trijata galloping ahead of me. Sita continued singing.

'One fine morning, the louts will replace the royalty. Ram will turn into a puppet and watch them taking over with his mouth shut.'

He laughed again. 'The Immortals will shower jasmines from above to celebrate the honorary ruler of Ayodhya. The loser and his Ram Rajya!'

Lankesh clapped like a maniac. I stopped abruptly at the gate of Ashok Vatika. Trijata forged ahead and stood behind Lankesh.

What had he made of himself? Was this the same man who had come to me with an adventurous dream? The man, who wanted to build heaven on earth, was now on his way to destroying it! How could heaven be soiled by the tears of an abducted wife? I cringed, watching this vastly changed individual. A demon!

'Be my mate. Make Lanka your home. You will achieve all that you have never dreamt of.' Lankesh proposed, offering a night of regal luxury to Sita. When she didn't answer, he hissed angrily, like a cornered panther, 'Stop mumbling. The king is talking to you.'

Sita was traversing some other world, far away from Ravan. She hummed of short, thorny leaves and the dark soil cushioned with grass, stealthy fish in the streams and intense monsoons, lethargic antelopes munching sweet fruits and bitter ones, growls of the lions at night and footsteps of elephants on lazy afternoons.

The brother repeated the folly of his sister. Sita's indifference to his invitation was read as an insult to his might and crown. Lankesh was outraged.

'King.' Trijata's soft voice made him turn before he screamed himself hoarse again. 'She can't hear you – she is in a trance. In their country, they lose themselves in meditative melody when they pray. Awake, but away. She told me.'

Whether it was the presence of daughterly Trijata or the information she conveyed – I couldn't quite say – Lankesh ducked back. He found me standing at the gate, eyes full of remorse, and tried to walk past me.

'Lankesh, don't you understand the conspiracy of the Immortals? They are coming after you.' I tried to hold him back, with my heart in my mouth. 'Sita is a celestial trap. They are provoking you to fasten your neck into her loop. Free her and save yourself.'

Lankesh looked at me with disdain. Our gazes stayed locked until he left with broad steps. Disgruntled feet dragged my body back into my chambers. Sita's song continued like an endless saga.

Was her Ram thinking of the Ram Rajya they had birthed together? Sita didn't know. She only stuck to her part of the promise. In her imaginary Ram Rajya, she was united with Ram. Ravan and I shared a real roof, but the distance between us had grown greater than the distance between Ayodhya and Lanka.

*

I woke up with a jerk from a night of disturbed sleep. Did Sita just sing about a golden deer? I rushed towards my window to hear each word carefully. Her voice was out of tune. She recalled the restless eyes, shiny skin, network of horns on the head, velvety and shivering body, and long legs that jumped away at the slightest sound. Its tail spiralled in the air and came down again, tempting onlookers to caress its head and softly hug it. The golden deer was as funny as it was naughty. Fruits thrown at it would be swiftly gobbled up and leftover seeds would be thrown back at the kind donor. It would invite from a distance but would not let anyone get too close.

A part of me wanted to absorb each word of the lyrics. Another part wanted to shut the window and stop the music. Sita's descriptions painted a portrait of a fantastic animal – sharp, smart, astute and gorgeous. The words felt haunting.

Marich often told me about his fascination with the golden deer. During idle chats, he would sit down and watch me weave a garland of white flowers for Shankar. Skilled at sorcery, he fantasized about transforming into a golden deer once before he died – preferably for a cause that mattered.

'A Rakshas birth has many ugly struggles embedded into it. I will someday live the life of timid innocence, scurrying in beauty from one step to the next, coming right ahead to enchant the audience and fade into the horizon before getting caught,' he dreamt aloud.

I laughed. 'Why tease the viewers if they can't tame you?'

Marich chuckled. 'The golden deer is meant for the wild. Masterless and free.'

I didn't ask more. It was a beautiful little wish. With brittle white stones on the floor, he sketched a vivid image of the golden deer running through the dark forests, away from the world of attachments. It was painfully similar to Sita's descriptions. The images and words stored in my heart as delightful memories felt washed in blood, praying for justice and mercy.

Marich had been missing for a long time. Everyone whispered about it, but no one asked. I confronted Lankesh. 'Marich is a man of his own whims, with great knowledge of occult philosophy. He will be back if he wants to,' he told me.

*

'That was my second mistake. To want the golden deer.'

Sita's voice was no longer steeped in beautiful adulation. 'The beauty of the forest must be left in the forest. I wanted to own it, though it didn't want to be owned.' She expressed remorse, 'The human heart is both a fountain of light and a pit of darkness. That day while gathering fruits, I heard a delicate call of the gorgeous animal. Its hypnotic eyes were telling me something. Irresistible was its beauty, towing my heart behind its slender legs. I pleaded with Ram to get it for me.' She paused, her forlorn eyes revisiting the recent past. 'The punishment for the same I bear today, as I stand like the golden deer once did, unwilling to be forced into the company of the unwanted.' Sita wiped her face with the back of her hands. 'It is widely held that an object of beauty serves everyone's eyes and, hence, is possessed by all who can see it! This is wrong. I apologize.'

A swathe of black clouds soared upwards in the sky. Trijata was silent. Sitting beside my window, I asked for a big block of gold to be delivered to my study. I directed some helpers to prepare the alloys. Lankesh was happy to hear that I would be occupied with a new project, something that would keep my attention focused on preferred things and hopefully away from Sita. Before he could sit back and relax, Sita's pensive melody lingered in from Ashok Vatika.

*'Ram didn't want to go after it,'* Sita sang as I checked the density of the alloys. *'He insisted that this deer didn't seem like wildlife, that something was unusual. I didn't accept any excuse. I only wanted the golden deer. Just to please me, Ram left to conquer the beautiful animal, leaving Brother Lakshman with me behind.'*

✱

No one was allowed to enter my study while I was working. Though I never pronounced this restriction, Lankesh somehow understood and instructed the attendants to stay away until called for. I sacrificed food and sleep to turn the huge lump of gold into fine threads. They were melted in fire. Before they solidified, I bent their heads into shapes that served my purpose. The wires were entangled in the middle and towards their ends. My palms were scorched by the heat, and bruised while sharpening the metal. The clang of my hammers, however, could not submerge Sita's confessions. Tirelessly, I engaged, my hands doing their work and ears their own.

*'It had been very long since Ram had gone to the forest to capture the golden deer. The sun had set. My husband was nowhere. The noises from the forest were terrifying. I looked at Lakshman, but he didn't look bothered ...'* Sita's voice trailed off.

I held a corner of a wire beneath my toe and spiralled the other end tightly between my fingers. When I released it, the waves remained. A drop of water fell on it. I wiped my tears in haste.

*'By then, fear and guilt had made me miserable. I told Lakshman to go and look for his brother. Don't you worry, sister, no one can touch Ram – Lakshman's calmness felt more infuriating than reassuring. Little did I know that the shaitaan had entered my head.'* Sita was choking now.

She was right. Once Ravan entered people's minds, all barriers melted away. He had entered my mind too, without my knowledge. I thought I was taking independent decisions, when all the while, I was walking on the fine lace he had spread on my path. His theories felt unique, authentic and enterprising. I had started believing in everything he believed in. All responsibilities were mine. Everything changed the day Sita entered Ashok Vatika. No wonder Ravan was so uncomfortable with my attention to her.

I climbed the ladder to reach the top, with a bundle of wavy wires in hand.

'*Suddenly, Ram's voice came floating from the forest. Seeking help, calling for Lakshman to save him. I was afraid,*' Sita sang. My hands slowed down. '*I lost all of my strength,*' she recalled. '*My confidence dwindled along with my experience of having known Ram for so long to guess what he'd never do. And I lost faith in Lakshman.*' Tears ran down her cheeks. '*I screamed at him as loudly as I could, commanding him to look for Ram instead of sitting idle in front of the hut. I readied to go by myself if he didn't, and started picking up stones, sticks and whatever else I could find. Lakshman, my wonderful brother. I will never forget the hurt in his eyes.'*

Trijata must have got up from the step on which she was sitting to hug her. In Trijata's arms, Sita regained her composure. For a long time, I didn't hear them talking. Balancing my feet on the topmost step of the ladder, I spun the waves into a pair of curvy structures for cartilaginous protrusions to be wrapped on either side of the construction.

*'There were voices coming from the forest, of struggles and injuries. I panicked,'* Sita's voice floated in after a long pause. *'Lakshman insisted the voices weren't real. But I wasn't convinced. With his arrow, he pierced the ground, drawing a protective womb around the hut, requesting the earth to hold her child until the brothers returned.'*

Labour doesn't care about time or people! The child comes out when it wants. The mother cannot hold back. I could guess what must have happened next.

*'Lakshman went off to the forest to find Ram, warning me not to cross the Lakshmanrekha under any circumstances. No outsider could harm me, unless I dishonoured it. I wasn't listening to Lakshman. An hour passed. I was in a dismal state when a frail sage approached me, asking for food. He looked like he would faint if I didn't provide help.'*

Sita's revelations took me back a few months. Those were the days when Lankesh had suddenly planned a tour outside the country. He had been very distraught at the time, though he didn't bother to share his plans with anyone. When I asked, he gestured for me to keep quiet and stay away. There was only one person who could unsettle Ravan to this extent – Meenakshi. The girl was back with yet another disaster.

# 11

When the mind is corrupted, even a bed of feathers feels like a bed of thorns. The metaphorical thorns prick so deeply that one carelessly abandons the comfort of the bed, only to land into greater troubles thereafter.

*'My Ram was in trouble, so was the sage. I quickly gathered all the fruits I had in my hut, hoping for the blessings of the sage to support Ram and Lakshman.'* So linear was Sita's compassion. If only this crooked world were the same!

*'The brahmin approached to receive alms. The Lakshmanrekha raised a burning fence, blocking his way. Even his finger would not come through,'* Sita had reached the end of her song. *'He was offended*

*by our poor hospitality that humiliated the distress of a destitute. Without caring for Lakshman's warning, I stepped out to help a sufferer. I shouldn't have. My third mistake.'* The music stopped.

Trijata tried to console her. 'Why do you blame yourself, Sita? You did what anyone with a good heart would do.'

Being good isn't always enough. Being tactful is a skill. Learning from failures is a strength. Sita was dauntingly counting her mistakes, one after the other, slowly taking ownership of every occasion when she had failed herself. Along with her, I had also started to reflect upon my past.

So many voices, so many events, so many mistakes!

'Every person must know when to stop. Violating certain boundaries is not only dangerous but also a sin,' Sita confessed. I agreed. 'The wonderful sage with eyes full of wisdom turned into a wretched giant with ten heads, hands like handcuffs ...'

Trijata must have covered her mouth as her decibels rose. Unflattering remarks about the king were punishable. No one knew what the punishment was; they just refrained. Sita had no fear. Separated from Ram, she had nothing more to lose.

'Once I had crossed the Lakshmanrekha, its spell was broken. As much as I prayed for it to spring back, the mark started disappearing from the ground. Ravan hurled me towards his birdcraft. My screams were meaningless to his deaf ears.' Sita did not say anything after. Trijata must have covered her mouth again with her palm.

This was the last part of the construction: the eyes. I fitted emeralds between the gold and layered it with black soot from the fire. The green eyes complemented the golden sculpture, making it look vividly realistic. What a pity that I couldn't make it breathe. Exhausted, I fell to the floor.

When I opened the door, Lankesh was loitering outside, breathless with anxiety, unfed and lacking sleep, polite enough not to knock but pale with concern. A month had passed since I had locked myself inside the study, coming out sparingly and talking to none. He bolted inside to see what had kept me engrossed for so long.

The golden deer, sculpted with gold threads, greeted him with a silence that Marich wasn't quite known for. Its front legs were folded inside for the last leap, while the other two legs were balancing backward. The divine face was inclined upwards, its wavy horns reaching for the sky and green eyes looking beyond life. Lankesh shouted instructions for the ethereal structure to be installed in the heart of the kingdom. All my doubts dissolved into thin air. Marich was dead.

*

From our palace, we could see the golden deer basking in the sunlight, almost alive but not quite. Many times at night, Lankesh would stare at the sparkling emeralds. He faced it from the front, looking into its eyes with great sadness. He didn't know how to cry, and he couldn't ask for forgiveness. He only missed Marich.

'Let Sita go. Else, this is just the beginning.' He hadn't expected me to be awake. His fists hardened.

'Sita isn't worth losing everything for. Leave her alone,' I repeated.

'Let her go? And do what in Lanka? Be your pet and wake up to the mutilated face of a sister every day? The great Ravan!' We didn't know we had Meenakshi for company. Meenakshi, of course, didn't need permission. It was her domain, her palace, and she could travel unbarred.

Lankesh opened his arms to her. 'Come to me, child.' She walked backwards. 'I will avenge you, don't you worry. You will find them soon on the soil of Lanka, crawling at your feet for mercy,' Ravan promised.

'Action over words,' Meenakshi muttered bitterly and looked at me as if her eyes were the fangs of a cobra.

*

When Meenakshi had disappeared after the killing of Vidyutjihv, Ravan's helplessness turned into anger. 'Couldn't you have taken care of her when she needed you?' He blamed me. 'How could you let her go?' I chose to greet him with a comforting silence, sometimes assuring him that his sister was fine wherever she was, that she needed space to deal with her grief, that she would come back to him eventually – as a more evolved woman. Each of my assurances came true, albeit not in the way I had intended.

Meenakshi returned one day, just as suddenly as she had left us few years ago. She looked shattered and terrified, far from the haughty woman we had known. Her face was covered. We could only see her eyes – furious and resentful. Lankesh left his lunch and stormed towards her. She refused to come near him. With a lot of coaxing, he managed to get close enough to lift her veil. When he saw her face, he screamed and kicked the adjacent wall. Hairline cracks appeared all over it.

Meenakshi complained about two princely brothers in the forest of the neighbouring country, who had molested her and disfigured her pretty face.

'I will drown them all in the sea.' Lankesh shivered with rage at the sight of blood on his little sister.

Feeling deeply sorry for her, I had already called for the palace doctors. However, I traced distinct discrepancies in Meenakshi's account.

'Why would they do this? What was their conflict with you?' Knowing her well, I had asked the obvious. She dramatically fell to the floor and wailed that her family was now questioning her, as it happened always to womenfolk who were blamed for every misfortune, while criminal men loitered with their heads held high. Her plight was terrible, but she was hiding something. She continued abusing, crying and cursing me until her brother intervened.

'How could you say something so heartless?' he asked angrily.

Her conduct reinforced my assumptions. I didn't respond, just repeated the question. 'What was their conflict with you? How do you know them?'

Meenakshi grew savage; I could see her vile wickedness. 'The brothers share a home with a feisty woman. Sita,' she said without hesitation. 'That woman should be brought to Lanka.'

I was stunned. 'Why? Who are you to decide where someone should be?'

'Don't forget Meenakshi is the princess of Lanka and sister of the great king who keeps the gods in his grip. She certainly has the right to decide who goes where. If she thinks Sita should be brought to Lanka, she must have her reasons,' Lankesh cut me off with a tone he had never used before. Meenakshi winked at me through the vulnerable look pasted on her face.

'Sita is considered the most beautiful woman on earth. She was desired by the Immortals, before her marriage with Ram.' She scowled at me and stared at Lankesh. 'Of what use is power if the most beautiful woman isn't bedded by the most powerful man?' Meenakshi lured Lankesh into her ploy, encouraging him to separate a happily married couple. He kept a hand on her head with immense affection, his eyes shining.

This was her understanding of power! I was astounded. She seduced handsome, married men because it made her feel powerful? She was provoking Ravan to commit a tremendous sin, insulting me in every way she could. My warnings didn't reach Ravan. The disfigured face of his beloved sister was all he could see, her shrewd counsel cloaking his intelligence. The greatest of kings laid down his weapons before the disloyal.

'Brother, there is more,' Meenakshi added fuel to the fire she had ignited. 'This Ram is rumoured to be an incarnation of Vishnu,' she whispered. 'I have followed them enough to believe this is true. Vishnu, who shields Indra.'

Meenakshi did not need to say anything more. Right in front of my eyes, Lankesh discarded all good sense.

'Finally, Vishnu!' He got up, infected by barbaric euphoria. 'The shield of the lech Indra is at Ravan's doorstep. Since the Immortals can enter Lanka only as a prisoner or a slave, he has assumed a demi-human form,' he said, laughing, roaring and punching his thigh. 'If this is true, then slaying Ram would end the disparity between the Mortals and Immortals forever.' He hugged Meenakshi tightly, caressing her hair. 'Sister, you have done a great favour to your brother.' From over his shoulders, Meenakshi stared at me with a sly smile.

Ravan bustled with vigour. He began to spend more time inspecting and reorganizing the armoury. The soldiers were assembled and trained rigorously. Vibhisan was kept away. A shiver ran down my spine. All sorts of commands slipped from my hands. No advice worked on Lankesh.

# 12

'You shouldn't have crossed the Lakshmanrekha,' Trijata said sadly.

'I didn't intend to. I was only trying to help the needy.' Sita paused before adding, 'I think I will always do that.'

'What? Cross the Lakshmanrekha?' asked Trijata, irritated.

'If someone comes with a need, I will always try to help. That's my dharma. Whatever happens after, whether the person turns out to be a saint or shaitaan, is his dharma, not mine!'

Sita was stubborn about her idealism, which may not have seen success, yet its sanctity prevailed. It was easy for her to humour herself with utopian hallucinations. She had not given birth to children. I, too, perhaps was more spontaneous till a few years back. Had a handsome stranger invited me today to collaborate in return for an exclusive opportunity, would I be as excited? I doubt it. My endeavours would never risk the future of my children.

By now, I was a mother of three. We named them Meghnad, Atikay and Akshaykumar. Meghnad, the oldest, was born after a long labour. I howled like a wounded bull for two days, after which I numbed and Meghnad took over. The newborn, I was told later, had cried so loudly that it sounded like the clash of turbulent clouds shattering the sky. I lay aside, unconscious.

Lankesh settled for none other than Shukracharya, the guru of the Asur clan, as the royal tutor for Meghnad. Shukracharya taught him not only the secrets of warfare but also exquisite sorcery. Meghnad mastered the deadly weapons and strategies of politics very early on. Shukracharya was full of praises. 'Your son is a great archer and will surpass his family in illusion-warfare techniques.' Lankesh swelled with pride and announced a royal feast. The country celebrated its *yuvraj*. Whenever Kumbhkarn was awake, he spent more time with the children now. Meghnad was everyone's favourite.

'Mark your time, child,' Kumbhkarn would advise. 'The time you spend to slay your enemy should decrease with every subsequent attack. Your growth as a warrior will be reflected by how unpredictable your tactics are for the opponent. The speed is critical. If you have successfully induced shock but allowed time for revival, you are likely to lose a winning battle.'

Little fists of the three-year-old pushed the enormous clutches of his gigantic uncle. Kumbhkarn rolled on the ground, laughing, and got up again to continue the fight. Meghnad clung to the uncle he could wrestle with only once in six months, for a few hours. Around midday, they both proceeded for confidential meetings with his father to discuss politics and society. With keen interest, Meghnad tried to understand the issues – sometimes with a smile, otherwise with a deep frown.

'You didn't agree with your father?' I asked him once when his frown didn't disappear after the court proceedings. He was in my studio, studying. He shook his head.

'Why didn't you tell him?' I asked.

'I will,' he said, 'if I feel it's important.' He went back to his reading. He was nine then.

The sound of my experiments never distracted him. He insisted that sitting inside my studio helped him concentrate better. Those were his ways of stealing time with a working mother. Sometimes he asked questions about the curves of the tools or the shapes of my constructions. I stole glances, allowing him to prosper at his own pace. Unlike his father, he was calm and composed, rarely angry, humble enough to honour the servants and their masters alike. And he brewed secrets of his own.

'What do you talk about so much with Vibhisan?' I nudged him when he was a little older. I had seen them hanging around, talking seriously about various topics. From the disjointed words that flowed in, I could make out that they were reviewing historical wars. Vibhisan was the wrong choice for such discussions. Or rather, he was not the king's preference. The uncle and nephew also deliberated on Lankesh, me, the citizens, politics and economy. Meghnad wanted to understand everything from multiple perspectives. After debating his concerns with a creative mother and pragmatic father, he heard out his philosophical uncle's versions with a lock on his mouth.

'Why should I tell you?' He was taciturn. I chuckled; he didn't.

'Oh, come on, tell me.' I drifted closer, my arms brushing his. The tough ice was far from melting.

'You have taught everything to Akshaykumar, nothing to me,' he complained.

Where did this come from? I turned towards him, bemused. 'Did you ever wish to learn architecture and sculpting?'

'No, but he has received a lot from you. I have starved.' He sulked.

I sighed. The boy had his father's pride and sense of entitlement, though he was more open to expressing them. Conversations were easier with him.

'Inheritance falls on you naturally. Your mastery of illusory warfare doesn't come from the air, does it?' I said sharply. 'The rest, unless you seek, you can never own. Akshaykumar has his own passion, and you have your own. Why be sad about not owning something you never wanted?'

I tried to get up. Meghnad threw his arms around me. 'He gets to spend more time with you.'

I had to smile now. 'Isn't this jealousy too late for a teenager who is also the crown prince?'

'This isn't jealousy,' he protested. 'Between my training with the mace and sword or mugging up the intricate rules of each complicated arrow, I see Akshay building Ashok Vatika with you. Plant by plant, measuring the yards. I sometimes wish I could join you both. Your work is fun.'

'Really, you think so? I never thought you could be interested,' I carefully chose the words, relishing the hand girdled around my neck.

'I am not interested.' He shrugged. 'But Akshay looks happier with you than when I am with Father.' He looked away. I turned his head to face me. 'Does your father know this?'

'No, only Uncle Vibhisan does.' He started arranging his books.

'What else does he know?' The boy was playing games with me. I didn't mind them coming.

'Everything on which I disagree with father. And everything I miss about not being with my mother.'

He left in long steps, leaving me rudderless and wondering what Vibhisan knew about my son that I did not. Meghnad was ruthlessly ambitious, never settling with less and aiming for accomplishments that his peers couldn't imagine. His resume not only established his unrivalled skills but also his exotic tastes. On the battlefield, he stuck to the agreed war strategy, but his performance was more creative than theoretical. During the last battle with Indra's son Jayant, he shot an arrow that transformed into a hundred vultures before landing on his opponent and scooping out flesh from his body. Jayant fled for his life, with the hungry birds circling over him. He jumped into the river and waited underwater for three days until the magical birds decomposed into black smoke.

'Where did you get the arrow from?' I asked when he returned.

'I created it.' He smiled. 'Don't ask me how. I won't tell you. My magic is my magic, yours is yours.'

*

In the mornings, when his father was in the royal temple, dancing around Mahadev to the music of the damru, with camphor and sandalwood smoke emitting from the huge lamps in both his hands, Meghnad would tag along to play the cymbal with gusto. On one of those days, I was startled to find the boy sitting at the entrance to my chambers, while I was worshipping Shankar at my bedside temple. He reminded me of Marich.

'Come inside, what are you doing there?' Meghnad didn't answer but stepped inside.

'Why are you here now?' I frowned.

'Just because I worship Mahadev doesn't mean I can't seek the offerings made to Shankar.' He took a bite of the fruit before Shankar and ran away. I giggled. Should his father know that his teeth had touched any morsel before the prayers at the royal temple were over, he might have them broken!

After a few years, he demanded of me to create a special chariot that could become invisible at its owner's will.

'I should be able to see everyone and everything, but no one should see me. The chariot itself will be a weapon.' A royal command from the crown prince – I invested my heart into it.

The chariot had auspicious symbols inscribed on its outer side. On the inner walls, I rivetted large sockets to hold war ammunition. A pole on the side displayed the large golden emblem of Lanka. I entered the vehicle for a test ride before the final handover. As the chariot soared higher, my creation passed a note of caution. Meghnad, seated on this chariot, would easily overpower the gods, Asurs and humans. However, if he ever confronted someone who had negotiated greater sacrifices and hardships in life, the chariot might change its loyalty and Meghnad could be in danger.

Magic has a mind of its own. It brings a thousand rewards but bestows few critical drawbacks as well.

I called for Meghnad and revealed the terms of the chariot. I taught him the chants to change colours while inside the chariot, that would dissolve him into his surroundings. The boy was overjoyed. He spent the whole day with his new device, studying the symbols on the outside and reading the inscriptions inside. He referred to fat books and scribbled calculations while preparing to exploit the allegory to his advantage. Within a few hours, he had mastered the personality of the chariot.

Ravan summoned Meghnad soon. Both father and son were thrilled to conspire an attack on Indralok.

Meghnad ascended to the sky riding on his chariot while I looked on, waiting for updates. On his way, he faced resistance and fought many Immortals. No one could stand a chance against him. In no time, he was facing Indra. Riding through the sky on his elephant Airavat, Indra constructed a wall of thick clouds between the Devas and Asurs. Meghnad was invisible to his enemy, but he couldn't see anything either. Layer after layer, the thick clouds mocked at him. Meghnad's targets brought down no more than dead stars. Laughter reverberated through the air at the plight of the terrestrial prince. My son was not one to get agitated easily. A fountain of arrows shot up to create heat in order to melt away the clouds. Heavy showers washed the earth. The sky seemed freshly cleaned, leaving everything transparent. Meghnad remained invisible. Lying before Indra was a decimated Jayant, chopped into several pieces and packed inside separate sacks. His head peeped out from the stringed mouth of the one of the bags, seeking liberation from immortality!

Severely shaken, his hands and feet trembling, Devraj dropped his weapons. He slumped down from Airavat and surged forward to help his son. Jayant in the sacks transformed into fifty Meghnads with swords, standing in two concentric circles with Indra in the centre. The inner circle of twenty figures guarded the escape routes and imprisoned the deity with enchanted ropes. The outer circle dismissed anyone who came to help Indra. When no one was left to fight, Meghnad seized Indra and chased everyone away from Indralok, finally avenging Ravan's fall under Indra's *vajra* many summers ago. He returned amidst gala celebrations with Indra as the prisoner of war, and Indralok transformed into an abandoned ghost-land. The citizens of Lanka cheered loudly. 'No world beyond Lankesh.'

Ravan was ecstatic with joy. The world renamed Meghnad as Indrajit, the one who had conquered Indra. I watched him from a corner as Lankan aggression was idolized. Indra was dumped into the dark prison deep under the sea. The coveted construction had been waiting for its occupant for a long time.

All of Ravan's dreams were coming true. I was happy for him.

The celebrations went on for days and nights. The golden country feasted and burped; even the birds and reptiles refused to sleep. Loud beats of drums evoked exotic dancers – their voluptuous bodies covered with fine silk and mogra flowers wrapped around their knee-length braids. The bells of their anklets rang out in the sky. 'No world beyond Lankesh!' The people cheered louder.

One of those nights, when everyone had slept after the festivities, I slipped away alone towards the backyard pool. There were no guards. Ferocious crocodiles and nasty sea fish were shooed away. I stood quietly before Indra's prison, the darkest and deadliest of all my architectures.

✱

'What brings you here, queen?' There was no animosity in Indra's voice. He was at ease, not angry.

Why brings you here, Devraj?' I asked him. 'Is my son really so skilled, or is the king of Devas so weak?'

The man behind bars was quick to respond. 'Indeed. Indrajit is very brave and skilled with his weapons. He has truly defeated Indra, but not solely through his arms. The warrior has gained control of his senses. He is liberated from the illusions of impulse.' On my left foot, a water snake coiled up like a toe-ring. Some ornaments were better cast off. I looked back at Indra's blurry outline, faintly visible in the darkness.

'Indrajit was not born in a day, queen. The idea of *Indrajit* took a lot of time. Ravan wanted

Lanka to be Indrajit – the place where Indra can be enslaved, and the *indriyas*, the senses, can be controlled. Where theoretical sciences are taught, but independent discoveries are discouraged. Where natural resources are exhausted by overproduction. Here, man must work like machines. Professional growth is welcomed, and personal growth is deemed sinful.'

Now a prisoner should criticize the hammer and the nails used to construct the magnificent Lanka! The tail of a dog can never be straight. 'So, you mean the work I have done all my life was no more than propaganda?' I flared up.

'Not yours, but Ravan's. Propaganda indeed,' he insisted.

'Don't forget that the people in Lanka are happy,' I uttered angrily. 'Happiness doesn't come by chance. We worked hard to make it happen.'

'Yes, they are,' Indra agreed. 'They have been conditioned to believe that ignorance is bliss. They must learn, but never question their learning. They must be devoted to the royalty with null criticism. They should not discuss the evident discomforts. In other words, incomplete feeling is the complete abolition of Indra. Lanka has long been on the path of becoming Indrajit. It only climaxed with Meghnad.'

The exchange with Indra was infuriating. I was especially upset with the last sentence. 'What do you mean by that?'

Wild frogs croaked aloud in the sea, and the snake coiling around my feet slid away in search of food. 'Only four people were exempted from Ravan's grand ploy of conquering Indra.'

'Who?' I asked sceptically.

Indra shook his head; droplets of water sprinkled around him. 'You. Surpnakha. Vibhisan. And Ravan himself. Ravan needed his indriyas to be active in order to deprive others of it. He overlooked Surpnakha and Vibhisan, thinking they would never betray him. You, he could not overpower completely, as much as he wanted to.'

# 13

It would soon be high tide. I could feel the upheaval in the sea. The prisoner was playful. He lounged in the water like he was fondling a pet – loving the waves, letting them pass, smiling at their vitality. I was getting anxious.

What happened to the weather? Why is it getting turbulent, I whispered to myself.

He heard me. 'This is nature expressing its jubilance, queen. It is about to meet its creator.'

The waves rose to his cheeks. He lowered his face to kiss the water. Froth sprang up and bundled on his head like a crown. The sea rebelling was not a good sign. Our control systems were not working. This was not possible.

Our captive was enjoying his detention. 'Brahma is on his way to earth to negotiate my release. Ravan has been informed. The gates of Lanka are being lifted.' Indra bent his torso forward, his hands still shackled. 'Everyone will meet their ultimate father. Insects, birds and animals are the first to register his presence. Other tribes are always the last.' He noticed many doubts swirling in my eyes. 'Boastful Mortals refuse to acknowledge bare, unpretentious clues until it is too late.'

An intense wave slapped across my face. 'Why am I not surprised? The Devraj always has a saviour attending to him, whether it's Vishnu or Brahma. Ravan never had Vishnu or Brahma at his disposal. He helps himself,' I rebuked the shameless one. 'You created Indralok with the Immortals and received the blessings of the best. On earth we have a grand Lanka, built by and for the Mortals, without any of your celestial privileges.'

Indra laughed. 'Ravan wanted Indralok on earth without knowing what on earth is

Indralok. What you created is its opposite, Queen Mandodari.'

'Really?' I mocked. 'What is Indralok, Devraj?' The sky was not visible from here. The flickering light of the torch cast obnoxious shadows on the prison wall.

'Everything Lanka is not,' Indra returned sarcasm for sarcasm. 'Time and again, queen, many have tried to understand Indra and acquire Indralok. The foolish believed that the Devraj possesses and protects Indralok as his personal treasury. The truth is, Indra would like to find Indralok wherever he looks. Resistance comes from the Mortals.' He inhaled heavily and exhaled over the waves. 'The Mortals choose to perceive only a fraction of their vastness.' The waves rose to hug him by the neck. He waited for the intimacy to subside. 'Ravan doesn't believe in generosity. The more he gives away, the larger he will become. But, in your land, the subjects are made to believe there is *no world beyond Lankesh*! So small is your grandeur.'

A droning sound made its way downwards. Indra was silenced for a while. Brahma must have reached the earth, I deduced, wondering how his conference with Ravan would transpire. The noise petered out. Indra cleared his voice. 'Mortals interpret Indralok through their shortsighted conceptions of beauty. They create perishable structures with expensive materials that corrode with time and interfere with nature.' He contemplated.

The jugglery of words was mind-boggling. In silence, I allowed the allegations to pass before emerging from them to fight it out again. 'For the Mortals, Devraj, Indralok is a misleading and chaotic fantasy, now dismissed by Indrajit.'

'Indralok is an emotion, queen. It is a magnificent myth. It can never be dismissed, not even by the triumvirate.' A surge of waves rose and fell, pushing me up against the wall of the underground cell. 'If Lanka were an equivalent of Indralok, the king of Lanka would not have to conceal his overwhelming love for his wife.'

I took me a while to recover this time. 'What …?' I could not say more. I did not know what to say. My voice sounded like the falling sand of an hourglass. Why should Indra bring this up? It was personal.

'Ravan fell in love the moment he saw you, Mandodari. His unbending pride saw love as an obstruction and weakness. When Indralok came walking to him, the poor king couldn't discard his cloaks of arrogance. He turned away from the pinnacle of pleasure, reluctant to offer humble submission to his beloved.' The red fish flocked to his waist. Indra didn't have any grains to feed them. He drew in his stomach and released it suddenly. The fish dispersed in haste, only to hurtle back in. 'Ravan's love triggers him to give without losing the custody of the gift. He persuaded himself that his heartfelt love for his wife was no more than a long-lasting infatuation. Can you think of anyone more unfortunate?'

'Ravan has more wives stationed in the majestic chambers of the palace.' I forced out a counter, my face flushed red. 'There are many mistresses living in his best-laid residences.' My wedding with Lankesh was for a fair cause and had been reasonably passionate. There ended the discourse. Why was Indra telling me something else?

'Go into the world and ask about Ravan's wife.' I heard the Devraj smiling gently. 'They are aware of Ravan's womanizing. When you ask for his wife, however, they only know Mandodari. No one knows who else he married or with whom he slept. Your husband is not loyal to you, but he is committed to none other but you.'

Some caskets are better left unopened. Not every jewel is suitable to all. I had no interest in delving into this *love* aspect between my husband and me. Indra was talking a lot. Before I could stop him, his verbosity cascaded again. 'The greatest of the kings is imprisoned within his own constraints.'

'He is not a prisoner. You've lost your mind, Devraj.' I wanted to whip the man in front of me. 'Lankesh loves his sister unconditionally. It shows. He poured everything inside his heart for Meenakshi. Who he loves, to what extent and how he makes it known, is his choice.'

Indra nodded his head, partially in agreement. 'That is exactly his prison, queen. His love for Surpnakha. He is aware of how emotional he gets about her. So he refuses to acknowledge everyone else.'

*

The sea had become exceptionally calm. My head was spinning, all thoughts jumbled into a bottomless whirl. Sea creatures were nowhere to be seen. Indra was right: animals were faster in responding to the clues of nature. I could feel mild vibrations stirring somewhere. There was no sound or motion, yet something was about to happen. I looked at the silhouette before me. Indra was watching me, too.

'Leave, Queen Mandodari, it is time.' Our captive awaited his release. I clutched a corner of my clothes within my fist.

'Whatever Indralok stands for, how identical Lanka is to that cosmic fancy – they don't matter, Devraj,' I said before parting. 'Our war has a clear vision. It is an armed conflict launched by the intelligent against inequality. Ravan is a significant representative in generations to call out the arbitrary difference between the Mortals and the Immortals. The uprising will be remembered.' Indra tried to mumble something, perhaps to defend the distinctions on Brahma's creative platter. I raised a hand up in the air. 'Hear this loud and clear, Devraj Indra. Ravan's story will rise to immortality even if his life doesn't. This is the oath of a wife. No world beyond Lankesh!'

*

I came back along the same path I'd taken to meet Indra. Massive waves pulled me behind with all their might. I held my breath and swam forward, fighting the monstrous currents by rising atop at times and diving below when the water surface was more tumultuous. When I reached the edge of the palace pool, my shoulders were aching. Arms and legs threatened to fall out from their joints. I knelt on the ground, gasping heavily. A loud blast reverberated in the middle of the sea. The dry grounds creviced. Salty water spiralled upwards and fell with immense force, littering the coasts with discarded shells and ravaging the roads of the country. Sea creatures dragged from the depths and thrown ashore, were left convulsing before they succumbed to their injuries. Flotsam hurled into the air along with broken pieces of iron and stones. They came back to hurt the citizens, crushing their heads and piercing their arms. My coveted underwater prison shattered into smithereens. The mountain of cobalt spinel within which the grand prison was constructed had gone traceless. A bottomless fissure stood in its place.

Indra had made his way out.

'Why did you say that Lanka has *climaxed with Meghnad*?' I had asked Indra before stepping out. His voice echoed from below as I stood unwavering at the topmost plank of the underwater stairs.

'Every deed leaves its impressions on earth.' Indra had said. 'The impressions inspire the next set of circumstances. With Meghnad, Ravan has reached the peak of his liberties. Whatever he does now will only bring his downfall. The Mahakaal will send his emissary to dismiss everything that Lankesh has tampered with, believing himself to be as powerful as the one he worships.' He stopped and drew a deep breath, sending ripples through the water. 'Be very strong, queen. When the calmest one performs a raging *taandav*, he can neither protect nor restrain. Whatever falls under the dancing foot perishes like they never existed. Mahakaal has begun his descent. This would be the time for tough paybacks.'

Mahakaal. The divine time, the wondrous destroyer, the terrific transformer. Mahadev. I let my head fall before Shankar in my small temple and remained there for a long time. Outside, our world had been jolted. The discharge of Indra hadn't gone down well with either Ravan or Meghnad, so what if Brahma had mediated. It must have been a hard bargain. Lankesh must have asked for favours that would corner the clans of Dev and Danav alike. The Asur would rise by novel parameters in some mysterious ranking. Who knows what else.

Mahakaal descended many autumns after! The largest one appeared in his smallest form. By then, our lives and my pride had taken chaotic turns. My wonderful sons were brimming with youth. Sita had stepped inside our premises. Ravan was a changed man. Meenakshi did not flaunt herself any longer; she mostly stayed locked inside her chamber. Kumbhkarn did not laugh so much when he was awake. Vibhisan was more withdrawn than ever before. The few grey stands on our heads reminded us of the long time we spent together, and also of the lost opportunities of being together! Only Sarama travelled from door to door, nursing the disparate wounds of the family and balancing familial ties.

*

A beautiful little monkey called in a thin voice, as if he was a child. The kind of melody I longed to hear inside my chamber but it had long disappeared since Meghnad, Atikay and Akshaykumar had grown up. He called me 'Sita'! I stretched out my hand. The monkey happily climbed up onto my palm, rubbed his nose and tickled with his tail, looking up at me with awe. Tiny eyes blinked rapidly. With great joy, the creature hopped onto my palm dangerously. I placed my other palm beside him for support, lest he slip. Delighted by this simple gesture of affection, the monkey stretched his legs and lay down flat, crawling and rolling in glee. 'Sita ma!' he called again, raising both hands to touch his forehead. My heart skipped a beat.

In Lanka, no one outside the royal premises knew Sita, and if they did, they didn't mention her. She was a controversial name in the political corridors of the country. The masses didn't dare to intervene. Where did this little monkey come from, calling out for Sita? Something was amiss. We were not worried about things going wrong in Lanka. But things happening without the knowledge of the king were unsettling.

'Ram would never give up. He will find a thousand paths that Lankesh wouldn't know of in his own country. Lanka will have to suffer the sins of its king.' Sita's curses had shaken me then, and they shook me again. On the soft of my palm was the first explosive.

'I am not Sita. I am Mandodari, the queen of Lanka.' I carried him to my window. 'The woman sitting there at Ashok Vatika is Sita. Take her away with you. Leave just the way you have come. No one should know. After this evening, Sita shouldn't be seen in Lanka again. Go.'

The monkey looked shocked. It took a while for him to realize that I was indeed not Sita. Rather I was someone from the enemy camp. The sweet smile on his face vanished. There was no more cuddling. He was up on his feet quickly and about to leap, when he turned and bent the knees to bow in front with folded hands, looking into my eye. I felt he was thanking, charging and challenging me all at once. In the next moment, he was gone.

I closed the window of my room, hoping that when I opened it again, Sita would be gone. Inside my chambers, I stood pondering deeply when it struck. Quietly, I exited from my chambers to walk towards the palace where Vibhisan and Sarama were conversing softly.

'Sarama,' I called from outside. She sprang up in surprise and came out, followed by her husband.

'Lankeshwari!' Vibhisan said warmly. 'Why are you standing outside? Please come in.'

I stepped inside. The couple always kept their arrangements simple and possessions minimal, which made it endearing to visitors. The walls supported creepers with colourful leaves and a vestibule that opened into the sea. It had to be repaired after the underwater explosion. They never blamed me or Ravan for the cracks on the walls. All our chambers were sea-facing, but Vibhisan's was unbarred without a formal gate.

Sarama declared, 'Don't leave without a meal', and disappeared to make the arrangements. Vibhisan sat near my feet, in spite of my protests.

'Can't you find yourself a proper seat like sane people do?' I said, embarrassed.

He smiled. 'Not when I am standing before Lankeshwari – the artist who transformed a piece of land into the sensational country of Lanka.'

I did not know whether he was really praising or it was sugar-coated sarcasm. People who spoke less and remained calm in adversity were difficult to understand. 'Vibhisan, I have come to ask you something.' I hadn't stepped in here for a casual chat with my brother-in-law. 'This morning I met a little monkey, he had come for Sita. Do you know about this?'

He looked up slowly and unapologetically. 'I do, Lankeshwari. That's Hanuman. He landed at my vestibule after crossing the ocean.' Straight and undiplomatic as always – exactly the qualities that made Lankesh angry, and for which Vibhisan was reprimanded generously. Old habits seldom change.

'This can be dangerous.' I looked at him sharply. 'Ravan would have you thrown out of Lanka if he gets to know.'

'I don't care.' Vibhisan was unrepentant. 'I just know that Sita must be set free. She is a bigger danger than anyone else. She is not a prisoner of war, only an object of lust for the reigning king.'

'Really?' I was getting agitated. 'Sita is not the only object of lust for the reigning king. Didn't you wake up too late?'

Vibhisan shrugged. 'Who am I to object?' he asked calmly. 'The women he brought in were happy to dwell in the luxurious residences allotted to them. You never said a word. Ravan visited them at his will. What am I to do there?' Impeccable logic. Uncomfortable, too. I wondered how to bring the conversation back to its context. 'Sita is the only one who is unwilling. She has not given herself to Ravan or Lanka. I shall go to whatever extent I can to stand by the woman,' he added.

'Do you know the consequences, Vibhisan?' The man was incorrigible. Never consulted me to help Sita; didn't think twice before compromising the security of his country. Only decisions, no plan of action!

'Everyone in this country will suffer the consequences if Sita is retained any longer.' He looked furious.

I was about to say something when a commotion outside alerted both of us. There were sudden screams and the sound of people running. Both I and Vibhisan rushed out. As the attendants ran helter-skelter in confusion and fear, we understood something terrible was happening in Ashok Vatika. Vibhisan ran towards the court to attend to Ravan, and I went to my window. There was a cyclone, worse than any storm I had ever seen. Trees were falling and attendants were running, some of whom collapsed due to injuries caused by the plummeting branches. My eyes found Sita. She sat in her position quietly, with a buoyant face unperturbed by the clamour around. The usual poignance was absent. Trijata wasn't anywhere to be seen. My face twisted into a frown. The monkey from this morning, now much larger, was jumping from one branch to another, raising a ruckus. He was breaking the trees and attacking whoever came in front. Before I could think ahead, Akshaykumar sped towards Ashok Vatika, with his sword hanging from his waist belt and a bow in his right hand. My heart sank.

I couldn't say whether it was a mother's heart or a woman's! Akshay was very sentimental about Ashok Vatika. He galloped ahead to protect the land from this invader. Arrows of anxiety shot up from my conscience. Akshay was fighting the one that had come to rescue Sita. I wanted to stop my son, but he was already out of my reach.

In a short while, everything subdued into stunned silence. A strange lull descended on the country.

# 14

I walked down the royal path, my legs feeling weak. The attendants on the way moved aside hastily so no one had to face me, even by mistake. I could hear sobs around me. I entered the quarters, where Ravan's howls were deafening. From his seat high up on the pedestal, he blamed the upbringing of the son who couldn't survive against a mere monkey. Meghnad had already picked up his weapons, promising to come back with the enemy roped inside a cage to be burnt alive. Fallen beside, Vibhisan silently wept.

A heavy metallic clang stopped them all. I had thrown Ravan's crown on the ground. He stepped ahead, holding me by the shoulders. I pushed him behind with a hard blow to his chest. He would have crashed to the ground from the unexpected strike, had Vibhisan not held him from behind. Meghnad came to hug me, I knocked him apart as well. He picked himself up and left with tears in his eyes. I could only utter, 'Release Sita.'

'I can't. This is the war I was born for, Mandodari,' Ravan murmured. 'I am not allowed to back out. This is my dharma.'

'Dharma! This dance of destruction is dharma?' I screamed so loudly, my lungs hurt. 'I want Akshaykumar back.' The mother's plight didn't touch the father.

'Ravan's son. The great Ravan's son. I had only sent him to fight a monkey. I assumed he would win this war at least. How could he fail!' The king of Lanka was mourning the loss of prestige, not the loss of a son. He stood before me with empathy, not grief. Obsession had rendered him immune to agony. He tried to come closer. I asked him to leave me alone and came back to my quarters. A series of interconnected events from the past flashed before my eyes. I cried my heart out thinking of the days when I could touch Akshay and speak to him. I wept for the bygone days and for the days that were yet to come.

Outside, the deafening calm was shattered by a huge cheer. 'No world beyond Lankesh,' played with the drumbeats. An attendant rushed in with news. After a terrible fight in which the monster monkey nullified every move of Indrajit, the prince had finally managed to tame it using the Brahmastra. The animal was now roped and pulled as a prisoner of war. The excitement of Lanka at the victory of their crown prince was infectious. Everyone forgot about the death of Akshay a few hours ago. Indrajit was the man of the moment. Lankesh stepped out joyfully to greet him with a grand welcome. 'The scoundrel will now learn who it has meddled with,' he roared. I kept staring into nothingness, recalling the one who was my son more than Ravan's, who had been my partner in creativity, who followed me with baby steps everywhere I went, who invented new tools for our architecture and who was not an expert in weaponry. He never desired to make Lankesh proud.

*

I had proudly told Indra that we were ready to make any sacrifices to establish our demand for equality. But no one is ever truly prepared to let go. The moment of sacrifice haunts for life. I was engrossed in the memories of good old days with dear Akshaykumar, seeking forgiveness from the departed soul for not being able to protect him. Behind me, Sarama sat in silence, her eyes flooded with tears.

'Sister, how could the monkey break through our security?' she whispered, taking my hand into hers. 'The codes you created in nature were everlasting. Even fish from the other parts of the ocean could not enter Lankan waters; they would get wrenched into invisible underwater wells. Birds from other regions couldn't cross our skies until the guards lowered the gates. So how could he?'

The dismissal of my carefully drawn security wall pricked me like broken glass from all sides. Bewildered, I scrabbled for support. My golden pot of water tumbled to the ground, its shrill noise reverberating between us.

'The security would have kept the rest of the world at bay, but not Mahadev.' I took a long time to admit, my heart trembling. 'Ravan and I had decided that if Mahadev ever visited Lanka, he should not have to seek permission or be stopped at the gateway.' Sarama hugged me from behind. I released myself from her hold. 'Today, Rudransh stands before the king, but he cannot recognize him.' I lamented. Sarama hugged me again, tighter than before.

Our tears blended into a single stream. 'Akshay was killed by an incarnation of Mahadev. He is in a better place now. Good for him, he left Lanka before all the destruction begins.' I got up, my eyes burning.

Sarama stood up too and placed a hand over my mouth. 'Don't curse the living, sister,' she uttered, wiping her eyes.

Loud squeals welcomed us outside. I couldn't tell whether they were of jubilance or fear. We looked towards the auditorium on our right. Mirrors installed in various corners of the kingdom were strategically angled with the glasses inside the auditorium. The celebrations at the royal palace were being broadcast to the citizens. All of Lanka was on the roads to witness the punishment of this cunning offender. Everyone knew what had happened at Ashok Vatika. It was a historic verdict against a 'shaitaan' monkey. The sentence had to be cruel and memorable.

Inside the auditorium, the monkey threatened Lankesh with dire consequences if Sita was not released and apologized to right away. Gone was the sweet little face and melodious voice that made me caress his hairy skin and long tail in the morning. When everyone dismissed his warning, he suddenly started growing. A group of guards went into a frenzy. The menacing figure grew taller and taller until his head hit the ceiling and surged higher, breaking the roof and emerging into the sky through the broken bricks. His height could put Kumbhkarn to shame. Indrajit's ropes had disintegrated to pieces. There was dust in the air. Fragmented stones were blown upwards and sideways, striking the bells of the central temple with loud clangs. Ominous reverberations from the swaying bells sent scary chills down the spines. The residents of Lanka ran from wherever they were, their trust in the king's abilities shaken for the first time.

'Indrajit couldn't tie him up in the first place.' The onlookers from Ashok Vatika gossiped: 'When the Brahmastra was about to strike, the fellow simply dropped his mace and bowed his head. A mesh of ropes fell over him as he kept his hands joined in devotion. The prince hurled the prisoner to his father, claiming to be victorious.'

Angry and frustrated, Ravan ordered that the monkey's long tail be set on fire.

'Don't, Lankesh,' I wanted to scream. My feet entangled within my dishevelled clothes and I stumbled to the ground. Sarama ran ahead, leaving me behind, trying her best to communicate my message to the king. It was too late. I could see fire in the auditorium, amid the cheers of the brainless. They were delighted thinking the monstrous animal would be taught a lesson. The monkey waited patiently for everyone to have their share of fun. He glanced comically at the faces seeped in vengeance, when he spotted me storming forward. The Mandodari he had met in the morning was a queen; the one he saw outside the auditorium was a woman who had lost her favourite child.

I saw sympathy in his eyes.

'There is no greater humiliation than the sympathy of the enemy,' Lankesh had told me many years ago. I halted abruptly on the path. Who was this monkey? Was he the god I worshipped? Was he Rudransh? Or was he Hanuman, a spy from the enemy camp who had destroyed so much of everything I had singlehandedly created?

An enemy is never kind. Mahadev had forsaken us. I stared sadly at the monkey and he stared back at me.

His tail was set ablaze. The fire was looming high. Those who had been assigned this task rejoiced, having finally maligned the ghastly creature. 'No world beyond Lankesh,' they shouted. All cheers and chants hushed by their own when Hanuman bolted upwards with his burning tail, sending everyone in awful hysteria. He sat on the topmost plank of the defence tower overlooking the sea. The fire turned the glass panels black before splintering them into pieces. With a single leap, Hanuman reached the structures on the left, where miniature wall sculptures depicted my meeting with Lankesh in the forests of Mandore. The corners were on fire now, ironically exposing the fate of our strange love story. Taken aback, the attendants ran to fill buckets of water. Indrajit let out a war cry and charged ahead to stop the monkey. Hanuman was now perched on top of the golden deer. I froze. When the living were on the verge of death, why mourn for those who had already crossed over to the other side?

Smoke was everywhere. Hanuman leapt ahead, destroying more. Our soldiers ran behind him. The panicked citizens caused stampedes. No arrow from Indrajit could restore normalcy. Ravan's sword couldn't perform any wonders. After the gardens and museums were destroyed, he demolished the centres for scientific experiments and Ayurveda on the outskirts.

'Jai Siya Ram!' he chanted thrice before diving into the ocean and disappearing for good. Lanka lay ransacked behind.

The damage was devastating, Ravan's roars were worse than that. He vowed to uproot the opponent; not a single person would stay alive to pass their filthy blood to another generation. Inside my private abode, I heard the ten heads of an illustrious king, whimpering like a hundred wounded tigers.

'Let Sita go,' I pleaded again. 'The woman's wrath is returning to us as curses. Release her.'

'Would you still stay put to that, Mandodari?' Ravan thumped on the floor angrily. His enormous pride was bruised further by the persistence of his loyal partner. 'I would have perhaps considered, had they come and apologized for what they had done to Meenakshi. Now, things will end only over Ram's dead body.'

'Meenakshi foresook her rights by forcing herself on married men. She initiated an attack on Sita because the men were not interested in her.' I tried to reason with him.

'Meenakshi is a child—' Ravan started. I cut him short.

'No, she isn't. She was not a child when she was with Vidyutjihv, and she is not a child now. You are a king first, a brother later. Be fair in your judgement. One sin shouldn't call for another. By all means, fight for Meenakshi. But do not deny her contribution to the mess. Go ahead and exact revenge on Ram and Lakshman. Sita is innocent. Why is she here then? Release her.'

Ravan looked away. Logic cannot mend a raging heart. 'This is not about Meenakshi or Sita,' he nodded left and right vigorously. 'This is about Indra and me. Vishnu, disguised as Ram, has interfered again.' He gritted his teeth. 'It doesn't matter who started the conflict; what matters is how it was addressed. I will return the intervention by disrupting Ram's life. He will remember this till his last day on earth. I will not back down.'

His fingers gripped my shoulders. Lankesh looked dejected. I leaned my back against his chest, he wrapped his arms around me. The deity may have disowned his devotee, but I hadn't partnered the man only for good times. 'The hurt dignity of the golden country will be restored,' I promised. 'I will rebuild everything, in less time than I took originally. The work will begin tomorrow. The defence tower and the sea security will be the first to go up.'

Ravan turned me towards himself, his eyes half wild, as if he couldn't believe what he was hearing. He buried his face in my neck, hurting us both. Those like Lankesh didn't mourn or pray for mercy. They only forced and fought. The world wondered why they were desolate in spite of their colossal achievements. How would the myopic thinkers know that those accomplishments were copper coins thrown in a begging bowl by destiny? The real destinations were denied to the dreamers.

'Where are you, the residents of Lanka?' Tillana went from street to street the next morning, putting on a grand show to wake up those who had never slept through the night. 'The queen has returned to work. Shouldn't you too?' The citizens assembled soon, looking at me in awe. They rushed back to their workstations, cleaning up the dust and burns.

The ruins had to be removed before the actual work started. Akshay, my obedient assistant, was only memory now. I walked towards the sea, trying to ignore my late son's laughter from one corner and yells from another. While instructing the labourers who had joined me leaving their own battered houses unattended, I stretched my right hand seeking the blueprint. Seldom passing instructions and frequently roughing my own hands to help, I watched them fondly. The defence was back in order soon.

This, too, will not last. The strike had come from Mahadev.

I vowed to live as much as I could, with all who were alive but might not be in the days to come. Unlike the last time when the constructions provided surreal pleasure to everyone involved and nothing needed to be said, this time I rejoiced in the return of every slab, inviting the team to celebrate each milestone, brick by brick. The citizens did their best to hide their grief, as did I. Lanka was ready to fight back. 'No world beyond Lankesh,' they cheered. I joined them.

# 15

On my way back to the palace one of those evenings, I summoned Trijata. She heard me carefully and went back to Ashok Vatika. Before approaching Sita, she turned to look at me. For some reason, she did not want to initiate this conversation. I strictly commanded her to proceed.

'Sita, why didn't the monkey take you with him?' she asked.

'He wanted to,' Sita told her. 'I refused to go.'

'What! Why?' Trijata was shocked. I wasn't, from behind my hiding place in Ashok Vatika. I had expected Sita to say this.

'Why should I run away like a thief?' Sita said firmly. 'Ravan had deceived me. He broke my trust and committed a crime.' As usual, her choice was idealistic; she chose legacy over safety.

For some time, Trijata kept shifting uncomfortably in her seat, slapping a few insects between her palms or watching a warbler in the sky. She looked at me from the corner of her eye. I motioned for her to ask more. She wasted time gathering dry leaves between her palms, crushing them to dust and spreading them over her long braid. Her highlights. She inspected her hair and looked satisfied. I picked up a few pebbles to throw at her.

'Sita,' Trijata began before the pebbles hit her head. 'When Lankesh dragged you into the Pushpak, why didn't you fight back?'

'I did everything to push him away, to stop him,' Sita reflected. 'When I failed, I dropped my ornaments from the flying vehicle, leaving a trail of clues. It would aid Ram and Lakshman in finding me.' She pulled out a ring to show Trijata.

It had been brought by Hanuman as proof of her husband's friendship with the monkey. 'I did not want to die, though.'

'What does that mean?' Trijata sat down before her now, her eyes widening.

'Ravan could have killed me,' she said, looking at the ring. 'He was better skilled and armed. I didn't have any weapons, nor was I as strong physically.'

Trijata was now impatient, as was I. 'Wouldn't death be more dignified than being a prisoner in another man's land? Why didn't you kill yourself?'

'Why should I choose death because of Ravan's cruelty? Ravan is no one to me.' Sita surprised us. 'I'd rather live for Ram's love.' She no longer sounded frail, impractical and vague. Hers was a bright mind operating with great clarity, even at a time when she was being abducted.

'Justice is restored when the criminal is condemned. Not only by the victim, but by the audience at large.' She sounded unyielding, like a woman on a mission. 'If I died, Ravan's misdeed would remain under wraps. His dignity would be unscathed and he'd be acquitted in the paucity of evidence. I have to live, in body and spirit,' Sita emphasized. 'As long as I am alive, Ravan's fears multiply with every sight of me.'

'Fear!' Trijata could not hold herself back. 'You really think our king lives in fear?'

My heart was pounding as well.

'Ravan desperately wants to prove that though he brought me here by force, it is my greed that keeps me in Lanka.' Sita looked at Trijata, smiling faintly. 'If he is successful, Ram will be immediately vanquished. No war will be necessary. Ravan lives with the fear of failure. My consent is his biggest victory, my dissent is his ultimate defeat.'

*

The spine-chilling announcement arrived after some time. The defence tower sent messengers to report that a large army of monkeys were throwing stones into the ocean and progressing towards Lanka.

'Let them receive a grand welcome,' Lankesh chewed his words as he spoke. The army was already prepared. Indrajit moved with quick steps to brief the horse and elephant trainers in the army. The otherwise bustling Lanka was numb. Hanuman's destructive visit was still fresh in everyone's mind. The residents pretended to have forgotten everything. On one of those evenings, Lankesh went up to the terrace of the highest tower in Lanka. With his sword held high, he roared, '*Har Har Mahadev.*' Children stopped playing, adolescents were distracted from their studies, adults stepped away from their chores and businesses were halted. Within moments, the island of Lanka was chanting along with their king. 'Har Har Mahadev' rose up through the air. The melancholy of the country over the last few days disappeared. Few musicians took out their drums and started playing zestfully. Women and men broke into an energetic dance. The children formed a circle around them and clapped.

I sat for hours inside my abode, listening to the chants. No one came looking for me, and I didn't go after anyone either. Outside my window, Sita had joined the chorus as well. Har Har Mahadev! The energy had inspired friends and enemy alike, uniting them in ways they didn't realize.

In the midst of all the cheer, I sent for Vibhisan and Sarama.

*

'Leave Lanka, Vibhisan. Do not fight this war on behalf of the country,' I whispered. Vibhisan's tearful eyes narrowed. His elder brother had always been a riddle to him. Now he was worried if his sister-in-law was going mad. Sarama was in a state of shock.

'Are you provoking me to betray the king?' Vibhisan was heartbroken. 'I don't agree with Ravan on many counts. But I am not a traitor. For all these years, is this what you believed of me? You think I am an unreliable brother?'

'I am not thinking anything about you,' I uttered with acrimony, startling both of them. 'I say this for the sake of Lanka. One of us must stay.'

'What is this *one of us must stay*? Clarify.' Though he was hurt, he couldn't be rude. Sarama stared in disbelief.

'Lankesh will not be able to win this war. His beloved deity, whom he invokes to motivate his countrymen, is fighting as his opponent.' I felt tired and spent.

'I know,' Vibhisan agreed. 'Why would you ask me to run? Why shouldn't I fight for him and die?' Sarama let out a scream, breaking into tears. No one consoled her.

'Go for now, to come back later.' I sighed. 'Else, Lankesh will perish in every way.'

Vibhisan looked up at the sky, trying to hold back his tears. 'He provided for us, his siblings, when we didn't have anything. He'd attack anyone who said a word against us. I cannot do this to him.' His voice choked. 'He was never fond of me, but he did not turn away from me ever.'

I let the memory pass. 'Return the favour then.' I sounded ruthless and Vibhisan feeble. 'After Ravan's death, his beloved Lanka should not refer to him as a villain. His vision should always be celebrated, at least in this part of the world. May his passion be immortal, if not his existence. We owe this to Lankesh.' My voice was steady and unwavering. 'A new successor chosen by the enemy camp will paint Lankesh as an antagonist, just like it happened with Kuber.'

I gasped for breath. 'Ravan has committed a sin; he will be punished. But the sin and the punishment should not be all that Ravan is remembered for.'

The pleasant sea-facing chamber felt like a furnace with heat waves storming between the walls. 'Do you mean ... you want to say ...' Vibhisan was shaking now; Sarama was trying to hold him still.

I nodded my head, sitting like a puppet. 'Yes, Meghnad will go too. He will not stop till he has seen the end. The end will transpire only when all Lankan warriors are sacrificed.'

Vibhisan got up and rushed out. He crashed at the threshold of my door.

'Leave, Vibhisan.' I walked up to him. 'Go over to the other side. Promise me today. You will ensure that even in Ram's land, when they celebrate the victory of their leader, the people will not fail to acknowledge Ravan's brilliance and Indrajit's talent.'

'Are you made of rock?' Vibhisan broke down, mumbling memories and prayers. I could not hear him. I didn't wish to. Three people sat in silence on that dark night, together but detached. Towards the morning, when Sarama had slipped into slumber, I got up. A hand gripped my wrist.

'Why are you doing this, Lankeshwari?' My brother-in-law asked, his voice fading. I leaned against the wall behind me, lest I collapse.

'Have you ever thought, Vibhisan, what Lankesh had longed for all his life?' Images flashed before my eyes, carrying me from one stage of life to another as if I were watching them sitting on the deck of the Pushpak. My father. Mandore. Lankesh. Lanka. Meenakshi, Kumbhkarn, Marich, my children. 'All he has lived for is to impeach Indra and seek revenge on Vishnu. He may have been wrong on many counts, totally wrong ...' I paused to regain my strength. 'One opportunity is all he wanted, to get his anger recognized and respected. Lanka was built to provoke the Immortals. Sita is yet another provocation. In this scripted battle between Mortals and Immortals – Meenakshi and Meghnad, you and I, are unimportant bystanders.'

I wanted him to leave, but Vibhisan did not move. Sarama must have woken up by now. She lay like a corpse.

'Lankeshwari, don't you regret marrying the king?' he asked, his eyes flooding and face flushed. I stiffened.

'No, I don't,' I revealed. 'I have celebrated myself in his company. If it was not for Ravan, I would perhaps be producing layout after layout, trying to rouse the apathetic to my artistry. My art would remain in the dark, my journey would not be as legendary.' I forced myself free of his grip and ran out into the open air.

Vibhisan left soon. Sarama did not accompany him. He did not come to say goodbye. Sarama never came out again, unwilling to show her face to Lankesh, yet keeping our secret meeting locked forever inside her heart.

*

The war commenced soon.

'No world beyond Lankesh!' Those in Lanka rejoiced at the prospect of the enemy being massacred by their deft king. To boost morale, the citizens echoed slogans reiterating their power and the enemy's incompetency. Ram's troop was led by Hanuman from front. Our defence guards lifted automatically. When Ram finally reached ashore, the Lankans laughed loudly at the army of monkeys. Would all of them be like the one who set fire to Lanka? The question was written all over their faces. No one asked anything. They went back to sharpening their swords. The armies clashed soon, raising a constant smoke towards the sea where the arrows collided, and bodies fell.

That evening, Sita and I both looked up at the sky. Flesh-eating birds had started circling from above. Were these birds from Lanka or from the land on the other side of the ocean? Would they be able to differentiate between the dead? Were they decided on which flesh to feast upon and which flesh to mourn? Or was food only a need and taste, free from every other classification?

Every day a huge army of warriors went out for war – the young and the old, the innocent and the experienced, the beginners and also the veterans. Every day, they came back with fewer heads. Every day, little lamps burnt in the windows of the houses to light up the path for the deceased in case they still needed the flickers. The living awaited their turn.

Wails and screams could also be heard from the other side. In war, they fight and they kill. Afterwards, grief has the same language, the same tears, the same prayers.

One after another, they all left. The best and the worst in the country were levelled with the slash of a sword or the piercing of an arrow – our army generals, who had made us proud and the youthful soldiers on whom our hope was pinned. When Tillana didn't come to see me again, I knew he was gone as well. Ravan's children from his other wives gradually stopped coming back from the battlefield. My second son, Atikay, was the next to fall to Lakshman's fatal strike. When the women came to call me for the mourning, I sent them away. Lankesh did not enter my quarters.

Kumbhkarn was woken up untimely, much to the horror of his attendants. The desperation was now increasingly visible. He cursed Lankesh for abducting Sita and shouted expletives at an absent Vibhisan. Brothers! He came to meet me before leaving for the war. 'Bless me for now, sister. I will see you again on the other side.' He bid farewell without a tear in his eyes. His head was held high representing his powerful elder brother. He fought fiercely, terrifying the army of monkeys by defeating Sugreev, the son of Surya and monkey-king of Kishkindha, now allied with the prince of Ayodhya. Eventually, Kumbhkarn was eliminated by Ram.

Lankesh was devastated. His bellows reached the highest clouds and the deepest seas.

We get to live only one life at a time. Within each phase of life, there is very little to lose and gain. The rest are aspirations or hallucinations. Too many had already laid down their lives in the war, from their side and from ours. Sita had stopped singing. She only meditated. I went out sometimes to meet the familiar faces, diminishing rapidly. Babies were still being born. The citizens continued to invite me delightfully, seeking my love and blessings for the newborns. I smiled at them and they smiled back, none of us meaning anything more than a silent reassurance. Lanka was broken but the citizens were together, adjusting a balance sheet every day, calculating what remained and what was gone. They still believed that at the end of the war, Lankesh would emerge victorious. This faith was precious. Victory forgives all sacrifices and deaths. Off and on, the Rakshasis played their drums. The children shouted, 'No world beyond Lankesh.'

# 16

The only warrior in the universe to possess the three deadly weapons – *Brahmandastra, Pashupatastra* and *Vaishnavastra** – Indrajit slew a large number of soldiers during the three days of his fight. Terror washed over the battlefield in a way that even Ravan and Kumbhkarn could not inspire. I heard that he poisoned Ram and Lakshman with a *Nagpash* before exiting the battlefield one evening. A thousand snakes were tightly wrapped around the brothers. They were bathed in venom, their skin

* Three ultimate weapons of the Trinity. They cannot be countered and can cause mass destruction.

burning due to the acid as they choked for air. Garud, the eagle that served as Vishnu's vehicle, was an adversary of the snakes. He came to save the Ayodhya princes. Hanuman was also badly wounded. By the time they recovered, Indrajit had used the *Shaktiastra* to paralyse Lakshman for good. He had to be treated urgently with the *sanjeevani* herb, sourced by Hanuman from the north.

Any king would be proud of such a warrior. Ravan hugged Indrajit. In his red eyes, I could see a hopeless despair. Of losing his sons and brothers, relatives and trusted generals – to one devastating war. Meghnad was the only man breathing in the family, apart from Lankesh. I left the father and the son alone. Late at night, Indrajit entered my chambers.

I sat with my back against the wall that opened to Ashok Vatika. Many nights I had spent on this seat, sleeplessly, while the rest of Lanka snored. The only one who stayed awake besides me was Sita!

My eldest son tiptoed towards me. His calm footsteps had changed so much since the time when we were younger, and his clumsy presence kept me alert. He rested his head on my lap, with his arms around my waist. He breathed in his mother's smell just like he did when he was a baby.

'How is the war going?' I asked as affectionately as I did about his studies only a few years ago. For the world, he may have become Indrajit. For me, he was still Meghnad.

'You have no idea what a menace it is to fight an enemy allied with Uncle Vibhisan.' His jaws tightened. 'He knows a lot about my hidden tricks.' He drew closer into my lap.

'Who is the most difficult warrior from the other side?' I slapped him gently on his shoulder.

He smiled with his eyes closed, rubbing a palm where I had hit him. 'Mother, I saw the one who is going to kill me.'

With a throbbing heart, I pushed him away. He came back. 'Why didn't you kill him?' I asked, exasperated.

'No one would have survived the Nagpash and the *Shaktishel* one after the other. He must have made some life-giving sacrifices that I didn't. Now life is supporting him back,' my son whispered.

My hands moved awkwardly, brushing against his muscular arms. 'How do you know he is the one?'

'Remember the terms of the chariot you made for me?' His gaze was locked into the dark sky outside. 'In all these years of riding, I have learnt more from it. The vehicle will become defunct when I battle a saintly warrior who has practised renunciation for twelve years or more. I will die at the hands of a gallant fighter who is neither completely attached to life, nor completely detached. One who has nothing to lose and has lived more for others than he did for himself. The one who has not slept for years ...'

'What is stopping you from discarding the chariot?' I almost yelled, unwilling to hear the adulations for Lakshman. 'I will break it into pieces right away.' I tried to get up hastily.

'Mother!' Meghnad pulled me back. 'Sorcery always boomerangs. How can you forget the basic law?'

My eyes filled up. Meghnad had indeed surpassed me in his expertise of magic, learning what I didn't all through my artistry. Why did I miss this heinous truth? Sorcery always boomerangs! It did for me and for everyone else.

'The chariot has served me for very long.' Meghnad sat up, facing me. 'Even if I discard it now, it wouldn't leave me alone. A payback is pending.'

I ran my shaky fingers through his curly hair. He had my nose and chin, the build and complexion resembled his father's. He had Meenakshi's nails too – long and severe. He chipped them regularly and combined them with other ingredients to be turned into arrowheads. His eyes were his own, always searching for information and finding ways to put them to application.

'Forgive me, mother, for all the disappointments I may have caused.' He raised a hand to touch my moist eyes. 'Following father's wishes was easy because he demanded them. Why did you never pronounce your wishes, mother?' I did not have an answer. My hands were stiffening. The moon had started its journey towards the west. I gripped his arms in the same way I protected him once from rain and fire. Meghnad did not free himself. 'If I don't get the chance to say this again …' he struggled. We both were aware that he had uttered *if* only to make it easier for me. 'I was jealous of Akshay because he had you. I would have been happier to die as the dull Akshay rather than the ferocious Indrajit.'

My fingers formed a fist. 'Akshay was not dull,' I uttered. We both laughed, hiding our hopelessness. I lifted his face to hold between my palms. 'Why don't you quit?'

He was shocked again. 'Because a warrior never quits.'

I looked away, wiping my eyes. 'Isn't living more important than conforming to idle rules?' Meghnad held his head down.

'I asked Father to withdraw, though, and return Sita to Ram.' He sighed. 'The king refused flatly and wondered whether I have got scared. He suspected that I too would run away like Uncle Vibhisan.' We stared at each other, sharing all we knew about the man who made us, and now he was sacrificing us too. After a night of talking and reminiscing, his hands wrapped around me, Meghnad got up at the break of dawn. I kissed him on the head, wishing I could hide him from the world. Standing at my door, I watched my son until he walked so far away that he disappeared from my sight.

*

Indrajit didn't go to the battle to die. He fought like a lion. He first tried to get rid of his dearest Uncle Vibhisan, whose advice was immensely remunerative to the Ayodhya brothers. Vibhisan was well initiated to Indrajit's war strategies. Even before he thought of them, Vibhisan would guess his next move and alert Lakshman. Indrajit lifted himself skywards and vanished, baffling the warriors in the front, only to reappear straight in line before Vibhisan. Not that the uncle hadn't anticipated it, but this time he had not passed a warning. The *Yamaastra* from Indrajit's bow charged at him. Vibhasan closed his eyes to embrace eternity. The astra was countered by Lakshman, with Kuber standing behind him, both frowning at a teary-eyed Vibhisan.

Indrajit turned towards Lakshman. The Ayodhya prince, freshly energized by the sanjeevani, was unstoppable. Before the day ended, Lakshman slew Indrajit by beheading him with the *Anjalikastra*.

# 17

The golden kingdom must have sunk under the ocean. Other than the uncertain lashing of the waves on every beach, nothing was audible. None of the houses had lit its stoves, no children cried, no soldiers made merry while poisoning the tips of their arrows, no birds chirruped and no elephants trumpeted. There had been no worship of the deity in the central temple. Thick garlands of rich white flowers were scattered around, like orphans. The kingdom seemed deserted.

I was on my bed. Sarama, my friend and sister, must have been shedding tears sitting alone somewhere. Memories were dispersed like broken masts after a shipwreck. Wild hair flew behind as Lankesh strolled on the sand, facing the sea. Frenzied veins were embossed all across his torso. Prodigious waves came heaving from the sea and broke over his head, bathing him with salty water and blaming him for everything. He didn't move.

I and Lankesh hadn't spoken properly in a long time. I could feel the erratic heartbeats of the affronted monarch. As the hours passed, Lankesh pulled his hair behind, knotting it at his shoulder. The winds slowed down. Rising waves stopped mid-way and hurried back to the sea. The unfinished warrior raised his hands up, pledging that he wouldn't die until his last breath.

In a few hours an attendant came running at my door. 'Queen, come outside. The king is proceeding towards the central temple.'

Lankesh was about to host a huge *yagna*. It would make him invincible in his war with Ram. I hauled myself to the portico. Eyes red, muscles bulging out, chest pumped, hands closed, wet hair frizzing behind and a large red tilak on his forehead – Lankesh looked like a sacrificial animal walking himself into annihilation. He was in a daze. The followers carried huge lamps emitting fragrant smoke from burning incense. Baskets with white flowers were balanced on their heads. They filled the air, chanting, 'No world beyond Lankesh.'

The royal procession moved on to the central temple, their voices audible with the resounding echo of silver bells. I came back inside and dropped myself on the bed.

My eyes were closed. A sudden alert flung them open. There was someone on my balcony! I didn't react, pretending to be oblivious of this development. The intruder was in no hurry. The smell of the body wasn't quite known to me. He wasn't from Lanka. Could be a murderer from the enemy camp. I was not worried, though. My life didn't have anything left for me to fear death. But the queen of Lanka couldn't be assassinated by a random miscreant. I looked at Shankar. A sword was fitted below the bedside temple. I stretched my hands to feel it within my grip.

Between the balcony door and the bed, I cast a spell. An invisible sheen went up. If he'd try to come closer, he'd be trapped in an infinite loop till I set him free. Slowly, I sat up on the bed. The flickering lamp cast dancing shadows across the wall. A thin voice whispered from outside. 'Would I be allowed inside, *ma*?'

*Ma*!

Who could be so insensitive to call me *ma*? 'Who is there?' I called out roughly.

A young monkey, well-built and bright, appeared at the door. 'Why did you call me *ma*?' I charged directly.

Realizing he wouldn't be allowed to come too close, he dropped to the ground and joined his palms to greet me. I grimaced. He was one of the warriors because of whom I would never hear 'ma' again in this birth!

'Who are you? Why are you here?' Who knows what conspiracy had brought him to me. 'I am not Sita, in case you are mistaken.' I wanted to tell him to leave or I'd cut him into pieces.

He gathered himself at the door and sat down, folding his knees.

'I am Angad, ma. The son of Tara and Bali. Mother Tara had advised me to meet you and seek your blessings.'

Tara, the queen of Kishkindha!

Too many people had spoken of her. She married Sugreev, the younger brother of the mighty Bali, after the latter was killed through treachery by none other than Ram. Sugreev promised to mobilize the monkey-army for the rescue of Sita from Lanka. In return, Ram aided Sugreev in killing his elder twin and assuming the throne of Kishkindha. I grimaced again at the sinful liberties available to the Immortals. Bali was a legend. He defeated Ravan and yet they struck a rare friendship. 'He will make you laugh with him, and he will make you fall in love with him.' Lankesh used to talk very fondly about Bali, praising the charisma, humour and generosity of the erstwhile monkey king.

The day when the news of Bali's death reached, Ravan was crestfallen. He ran towards

Ashok Vatika with an open sword. 'Marry me now or die!' he bawled at Sita. 'Your Ram is a coward.' Rage and gloom poured out of his eyes like boiling lava. Sita cringed but looked away without answering. Trijata came running to pull me out of my quarters. I held his hand just in time, stopping the sword from falling on Sita.

'You cannot raise a weapon at a woman. Step back right now.' I stood between Ravan and Sita, trying to push him backwards.

Ravan looked at me furiously. 'Raising arms against a woman is a sin? Raising arms against Sita is a sin? Raising arms against Meenakshi wasn't?' His voice was bitter.

'Let me reframe,' I countered coldly. 'Raising arms against the unarmed is a sin.' From the corner of my eyes, I could see Sita's gaze locked on me. 'If you want to kill her, then challenge her to a battle. Equip her with weapons first. Let her defend herself.'

Ravan grunted in fury. 'Battle with her? This rag of a woman who cannot even stand properly?' He felt humiliated by the proposition.

'If you are unwilling to battle her, then you cannot kill her,' I said firmly.

Lankesh stepped back, still fuming and gasping. 'Why shouldn't I kill her?' he thumped his chest. 'Ram, her husband, is the incarnation of Vishnu,' he pointed at Sita with his sword, 'and has killed my friend Bali, for no apparent reason. No conversation, no negotiation, not even any introduction. Just an arrow, shot from behind the bushes, piercing the heart of the big, brave monkey.' Ravan did not have many friends. The death of Bali was a great loss for him. 'Integrity is only for the Mortals? The Immortals are free from all principles?' he scowled.

'No, Lankesh.' I remained standing between him and Sita. 'Integrity and principles are only for the believers. Mortals or Immortals doesn't matter.'

Lankesh threw the sword away. It hit a few trees and stilled. 'My friend's death will not be forgiven.' I touched his chest to calm him down. 'If Ram survives, he will also be backstabbed, in more ways than one. Mark my words.'

I pulled him back towards our chambers. Lankesh put up no resistance. I turned to see if Sita was all right. For the first and the last time, our eyes met.

*

I got up to sit on the throne inside my chamber, burying all the ruins that my mind was crawling through. Angad was patient and bold, almost as old as my Akshay. 'Why have you come here, Angad?' Fatigued with life and its memories, I wanted his answer to be as brief as possible.

The central temple was active now, abuzz with devotees and attendants crowding the base of the stairs. They were not allowed to venture further. The flowers were arranged, holy music played, the smoke and fragrance of camphor spread through the premises. The great yagna was organized with great vigour.

With our sons and relatives gone, was victory still important? Unfortunately it was. Ravan did not initiate his campaign for relatives and sons. So, nothing ended with the relatives and sons, until the pioneer discontinued the chase. Ravan would have to show up. The war must go on.

Amid the mayhem of the vibrant chaos consoling every bereaved mourner and ardent seeker, I heard the unthinkable. 'Ma, I have come to destroy the yagna. It should not be completed! I need help.'

Brief. Not a word extra.

If my eyes were spears, they would have chopped the monkey and thrown his body parts into the sea. But the eyes are far more resilient than the mind. Angad made no attempt to explain himself, silently tolerating the intense wrath directed at him.

'Is this why Tara has sent you here?' I asked after a long pause.

'Yes, ma.' He nodded. 'She said you will understand. If Ravan completes the yagna, this war will continue forever.'

'Leave, right now,' I stood up from the throne. My tolerance had been tested enough. Angad quietly got up and exited my sight. He didn't leave though. He waited outside my door, loitering in the corridor. The holy intonations from the central temple soared again.

The yagna. I gulped down a pot of water. There were only two possible situations: one was Ravan completing the yagna, and the other was interrupting his yagna. Would completing the yagna help Lankesh win the war? No, it would only make it impossible for anyone to defeat him. If Ravan cannot be defeated, then will Ram be dead? No, Ram was allied with the Immortals – he himself was an incarnation. The war would never end. Resource after resource would be eradicated. Other than the two warriors, everything would be blown up in the obstinate eternity of a barbaric war.

Conversations with self are always difficult. They expose all kinds of difficult truths. Harsh facts are topped with information that was never sought. Lankesh was on the verge of destroying life in Lanka. Releasing Sita was no longer an option. If the war was not terminated, we would head towards a catastrophic loop.

The war could be terminated only by ...!

The Brahmand looked at me, with hope and remorse. There was no one to consult. This decision had to be only mine. It would determine whether the future generations will be born amid a cloud of funeral dust or in bright sunshine. Where was the Indralok that Ravan had aimed for? We were headed towards hell.

I pulled out the hidden sword and smashed the temple first. The bed collapsed with the steady strokes. Whatever came in my way was demolished to dust. Dropping the weapon finally, I walked out of my chambers. Reluctant feet felt heavy, my eyes moist with tears. The view outside hazed and intensified at will. I felt sick. The winds mellowed, turning the land gloomy. I dragged myself to the central temple. Without a word, Angad followed me. He was not alone; there were other monkeys accompanying him. In silence, they leapt forward to keep pace with me, their hands clutching the branches of the trees one after the other, hiding behind the motionless leaves.

The guards at the central temple made way for me. The monkeys took advantage of the cleared path. Ravan was seated in an isolated place, his yagna in progress. No one else was allowed anywhere around. His backbone was as erect as it had been when I saw him first. The thin shawl covering half his torso had so many times been draped over us when we slept holding each other. The bulging muscles on his arms reminded me of the blue marks that appeared on my body every time he touched. He seemed to be smiling in a meditative state. The face was tranquil. Engrossed in solemn suspension, he recited his sacred chants. I stopped to watch him for a while, before shrieking at a high pitch voice, piercing the air.

'Lankesh! The notorious monkeys are here. They have destroyed my abode, broken the walls and now they are after me. They are teasing and pulling my clothes, they are molesting me. Help me, save me,' I sounded absurd. My tears were the only truth, everything else was a farce.

Ravan had entered into a trance that wasn't easy to break. The impeccable pronunciation of the mantras was hypnotic. He continued peacefully, sporadically pouring fuel into the great fire lit before him. I screamed again and again, howling my heart out and making a mockery of my misfortune. He didn't budge. Every sin has its punishment. For Ravan, sinning was perhaps a respite to force the denied attention towards his genius. I was to be blamed for standing by the sinner. I didn't have a single regret, only gratitude. For one last time I looked at the handsome man, immersed in seeking invincibility.

The biggest victory of a warrior is to defeat the forces that obstruct his faith in his capabilities. I laughed at Indra. Conspired by Angad – Bali's son and Indra's grandson – Ravan's death would be the worst defeat of the Immortals.

I screamed with all my might, complaining that Ram had crossed the sea to fight for his wife, while the great Ravan wouldn't rise to protect his.

Lankesh shivered suddenly and turned. He forgot that I couldn't be touched till I willed. He forgot that I could build a magical wall to distance unwanted intruders.

I fell unconscious to the temple ground.

# EPILOGUE

Ravan died doing what he believed in and lived for, call it his greed or goal. With his last breath, he attained his coveted immortality. Not on his terms, maybe, but immortality it was.

The merits of earthlings multiply after death. What isn't valued in a living body finds mention in cherished memoirs. Strange are the ironies of life. I gazed up. The sky was clear. The Devas descended to bow before him. Indra stayed away. Ram abandoned his bow and stood at the feet of the slayed warrior with both hands joined together. 'A great visionary,' they discussed, looking relieved, 'who attempted the impossible and almost succeeded.'

Lankesh lay on the smoke-filled battlefield with his lifeless eyes open. Even as a corpse, the spear was held tightly in his grip. The hawks moved closer; their circles above us were smaller now. Covered with the garlands Lankesh used to worship Mahadev, his body was lifted on the shoulders of both friends and enemies. 'No world beyond Lankesh,' the citizens of Lanka cried. Their faces flushed with tears, everyone in the country had assembled to bid final farewell to their beloved king. From the desolate gate of Ashok Vatika, Trijata led Sita out. The woman walked alone towards the camps on the other side, where the triumphant army celebrated Dussehra.

*

Ravan's pyre kept burning. The fire was never put out. I stared at the flames shooting high up into the sky, emitting black smoke that still smelled like Lankesh. After days of waiting, the others left, one by one. I did not go back to the palace. I prayed for the peace of his soul. I prayed for a befitting punishment for me. Would Lankesh know about my last trick now? Do terrestrial betrayals matter after death?

Day after day, the heat scorched my skin. I developed dark patches and wrinkles, the hair greyed faster. Ravan still kept burning. I didn't blink. The residents of Lanka approached me, seeking advice on what next and who next. The victorious warriors had not forced their representative on the Lankan throne. I convinced them that Vibhisan was their rightful king. Lankesh would have approved of him, should he be alive today and so would I. They bowed before the command and left, turning back after each step, wondering if I would be willing to return with them.

Vibhisan was crowned as the chief of Lanka but was never referred to as the king. My brother-in-law had done his job well. During his days on the other side, Vibhisan had used every opportunity to tell the enemy about the magnanimity of the Lankan leadership. Ravan, a dedicated dreamer; Ravan, the great warrior and a devotee of Mahadev; Ravan, the veena player, scholar and strategist.

Ram and his companions returned to their land. People there identified Lankesh as the mythical villain who wronged Sita and fought a devastating war with Ram. Researchers offered a thousand interpretations for Ravan's ten heads. The festival of Dussehra was repeated each year, honouring Ram's victory over Ravan. They burnt the effigies of Ravan, Meghnad and Kumbhkarn, reminding themselves that great power could meet a horrific end if karma was compromised. Remembering Ravan became compulsory at every celebration of Ram. The mention of Ayodhya would be incomplete without the mention of Lanka.

Ram Rajya was established in Ayodhya with great pomp and splendour, Vibhisan told me when he visited next. People there were overjoyed with the modern leadership which prioritized the opinions of the people. Sita and Ram sat on the throne together. Their dream had started yielding fruits. Good for them.

Vibhisan waited silently beside me, staring at the burning pyre for a long time. He held towards me a letter from Tara. I refused to accept it. I did not want to hear anything from Tara; I had nothing to do with Sita's life post her exit from Lanka. 'Hanuman has come to deliver the letter. Would you meet him?' Not that he did not know my answer. Standing behind him, the shadow of Rudransh crept onto the grass. I did not wish to see him. Hanuman lay flat on the ground, joining his hands together. When I did not return his greeting, he got up and left.

'What will you do here, Lankeshwari? For how long will you stay?' Vibhisan broke down, saying everything he could to convince me to return with him.

'Let me be, Vibhisan. I want to disappear into nonexistence.' I leaned my head backwards and looked into the eyes of my brother-in-law. 'No one should remember me, no one should know about my betrayals, no one should repeat my sins. No one should suffer an end like mine. Let Mandodari fade from the mortal memory.'

Vibhisan jumped backwards as if bitten by a snake. 'Mandodari will fade from memory? Lankeshwari, the creator of the golden kingdom, wants the world to forget about her? You think that is possible?' he shouted. I held his hands like the old times and made him sit beside me.

'Do me a favour, my brother,' I whispered. 'One last favour.' Vibhisan gasped, guessing what I was about to tell him. 'Don't ever mention who built Lanka. Help the future generations forget everything.' He tried to get up again; I gripped his hand. 'Do this for me, Vibhisan. Consider this Lankeshwari's final wish.' I waited for his sniffles to subside. 'Lanka was my only gift to Lankesh. I never wanted immortality, Lankesh did. Lanka was the guaranteed device for a spirited mortal to unsettle the Immortals. May all of this belong only to Ravan. May every appreciation for Lanka extend Ravan's immortality.'

Vibhisan closed his eyes. Tears rushed down his face. Slowly, he freed his hand and got up.

With slow, weary footsteps, he walked back towards the palace.

The citizens of Lanka started recalling Ravan as the irrepressible revolutionary who gave up his life and sacrificed his kin to manifest the grandeur of the Mortals. Ravan occupied his eternal throne even from the other side of life. He did not perish from hearts like Kuber. Lanka offered oblations to the inspiration who came from nowhere, made phenomenal contributions and retreated into a place from where no one returned. The ruins in various parts of the country were rehabilitated by the artisans and the architects I had trained. Shrines and temples were set up with idols of Ravan. Lankesh was worshipped as a deity.

I raised my fist up in the air and uttered our beloved mantra once again. The passing wind carried my voice, echoing everywhere it touched, through rivers and meadows, forests and sands, lands inhabited and abandoned.

*'No world beyond Lankesh.'*

*'No world beyond Lankesh.'*

*'No world beyond Lankesh.'*

# ACKNOWLEDGEMENTS

I must begin with the readers. Thank you for the generous response to the Sati series. For connecting with me across various social media platforms and expressing your delight. For raising questions and for recommending the works to more readers and forums. I am overwhelmed.

I must especially mention here the Instagram artists whose creativity mesmerizes me. The way you photograph the book/s on windowsides and tables, adjust the light and shade in ravishing proportions, add pearls or plants, spread zari or laces – they make for a terrific afterstory, which leaves an author humbled and grateful. You guys are fabulous. I am thankful for your reviews.

I am thankful to the very predictable life with magic at unknown turns, when sudden occasions and conversations (or the lack of it) reinforce ancient philosophies. They are recycled as resources in my writing.

Much thanks to Swati Soni for combing the internet to source relevant reading materials and research documents on Ravan, Lanka, Meghnad and Mandodari.

In the course of my journey with *Mandodari*, I am immensely thankful to the team of Pan Macmillan India – Isha, Rajdeep, Teesta, Elizabeth, Saburi, Ditsha, Santosh and Vijay. I can't stop missing Dr Prasun Chatterjee, with whom the journey had begun. Big thanks to Misha for coming up with the wonderful jackets for the books.

My sincere gratitude to author–economist Bibek Debroy for his tremendous support and encouragement. He is the knowledge bank that settles many of my confusions gracefully. Author friends – Ashwin Sanghi, Anand Neelakantan, Saikat Majumdar, Kiran Manral, Saiswaroopa

Iyer and Utkarsh Patel – much thanks for your constant support and for producing excellent work from your own tables, which inspires me immensely. Saikat, thank you for the beta-reading and the long conversations which make me think more critically. Senior authors – Namita Gokhale and Chitra Banerjee Divakaruni – I am a distantly placed learner with a voracious appetite for your books. Your writing is my homework.

Thanks to my mother, Ratna Dasgupta, for agreeing and disagreeing with me on diverse topics. Things that I want to tell her, but don't, sometimes slide in as dialogues in the stories. My husband, Tuhin A. Sinha, never reads my manuscripts till they come back in book form (and vice versa). But during the writing stage, we share ideas and hold debates, questioning each other's thoughts, ideas and ideologies. When Google fails to provide an apt synonym, he is my go-to person.

My son, Neev Tanish – I owe to him my writing career.

## ALSO IN THE SATI SERIES